Tongues of Flowers

> Kaylee,
> This book is not perfect. There are typos & some plotholes, but when I read it I couldn't help but think you would like it too. My friend wrote it, & you guys remind me of each other in some ways. I hope you like it! Merry Christmas ♡
> -Abi

Lynn S.E.

Acknowledgements

Any book I ever write, whether it's an article, a romance, or a tale with talking animals, it all goes back to Christ, in some form. Without God, everything I have, am, or create, comes apart.

I am very thankful for my family and must acknowledge them first. My parents and grandparents have made anything I ever create possible through their endless support. And thank you to my best friend who also happens to be my sister, she is the first to hear about all my ideas in their earliest stages. She also keeps my humble by roasting me incessantly, so yeah, thanks, Liz.

I wrote this book while getting ready to move to a new city, and I was a bit of a mess, so I must thank my friends, many of which are also my church family, for encouraging me spiritually and creatively; you know who you are.

I also want to give credit where it's due—many of you found me through Tiktok and decided to give me a chance, you play a much bigger role in these stories than you realize. Thank you.

And thank you to the fellow artists, writers, photographers, designers, and readers who helped make this project possible through their creativity, insights, and/or other resources: Liz, Lily, Lupita, Jarron, Abigail, Zerita, Leah, and Z.

Trigger Warnings

This book contains some heavy topics that may not be suitable for all readers. Please make the best decision for yourself. This book contains strong language, mention of homicide, mention of suicide, depictions of verbal and physical abuse, depictions of domestic violence, depictions of depression, body shaming, mention of child abuse, and mention of sexuality.

Dedicated to Mom, she works hard, gives generously, and loves abundantly.

Table of Contents

CHAPTER ONE: When Alba Met Ted 1

CHAPTER TWO: The Beginning and the End 4

CHAPTER THREE: The Raleigh Estate 7

CHAPTER FOUR: How Was I to Know 11

CHAPTER FIVE: The Seminarian 17

CHAPTER SIX: Take it Like a Woman 22

CHAPTER SEVEN: Tongues of Flowers 26

CHAPTER EIGHT: The Mischief of Isolation 30

CHAPTER NINE: Without Pretension 35

CHAPTER TEN: Truth's Safe Haven 39

CHAPTER ELEVEN: O Sacred Truth 43

CHAPTER TWELVE: The Apathetic Mansion on Main St 47

CHAPTER THIRTEEN: Checkmate 49

CHAPTER FOURTEEN: The Line You Walked 53

CHAPTER FIFTEEN: Passing Glimpse 56

CHAPTER SIXTEEN: Hampstead, NC 60

CHAPTER SEVENTEEN: Rays of Gold 65

CHAPTER EIGHTEEN: I Would Much Rather Be Wanted than Needed.. 69

CHAPTER NINETEEN: Cameo.. 72

CHAPTER TWENTY: The Little Chapel 76

CHAPTER TWENTY-ONE: That Night on That Bridge 81

CHAPTER TWENTY-TWO: Spirits Consumed After Dark 85

CHAPTER TWENTY-THREE: Nerah Lane................................... 88

CHAPTER TWENTY-FOUR: Lotus on Trapeze........................... 90

CHAPTER TWENTY-FIVE: Blue Lights in My Cage.................. 97

CHAPTER TWENTY-SIX:: A Pearl Under Pigs............................ 99

CHAPTER TWENTY-SEVEN: Poets Don't Cry............................ 100

CHAPTER TWENTY-EIGHT: Specs of Green............................. 102

CHAPTER TWENTY-NINE: Made for This................................. 105

CHAPTER THIRTY: The Ever-Unfolding Plan............................ 106

CHAPTER THIRTY-ONE: People Either Will Love or Hate This Part.. 111

CHAPTER THIRTY-TWO: Stay with Me 114

CHAPTER THIRTY-THREE: The Rigged, the Rabid, and the Running.. 117

CHAPTER THIRTY-FOUR: Wherever He Might Lead 120

CHAPTER THIRTY-FIVE: Until Planets Align............................ 122

CHAPTER THIRTY-SIX: Blessings, Eleo 125

CHAPTER THIRTY-SEVEN: Cabeza del Toro 127

CHAPTER THIRTY-EIGHT: Out Yonder, Where the Mermaids Cry 130

CHAPTER THIRTY-NINE: The Dynamic Duo Returns............. 132

CHAPTER FORTY: Tongues of Towns 134

CHAPTER FORTY-ONE: Artisan of Dreams and the Girl Hanging from His String... 136

CHAPTER FORTY-TWO: My Interview with Julian Wallace.... 139

CHAPTER FORTY-THREE: Spirits Don't Lie.............................. 143

CHAPTER FORTY-FOUR: The Transcript of Hakeem Brown.. 147

CHAPTER FORTY-FIVE: Doure's House for the Lonesome 152

CHAPTER FORTY-SIX: Votre Amour... 156

CHAPTER FORTY-SEVEN: You Know That I Know That You Know 158

CHAPTER FORTY-EIGHT: The Language of Dreams 161

CHAPTER FORTY-NINE: Me and You and All of These Ashes 163

CHAPTER FIFTY: Star Littered Views from the Terrace 166

CHAPTER FIFTY-ONE: The Call of Calls.................................... 168

CHAPTER FIFTY-TWO: Yoshida.. 170

CHAPTER ONE

When Alba Met Ted

The Widow by The Mars Volta

I met Ted Yoshida during the summer.

I was twenty-one years old. My copper hair was in a ponytail and some loose strands were sticking to my neck. It was late summer, so my skin had darkened to the point where people refused to believe I was a natural redhead. I supposed I had my father to thank for that, I never met him, but my mother described him as a smooth dancer from the heart of Mexico.

I liked biking through the rich neighborhoods because between the mansions and villas I could steal glimpses of the water.

I biked past Ted Yoshida's house, it was huge, of course. It was tan with golden light fixtures that looked like fireflies, and they had a private dock for their boats. Ted and some of his friends were drinking on the yacht.

I had heard of Ted Yoshida before. I had imagined he would be this serious, stuffy man in a suit. He wasn't like that at all. He was

Tongues of Flowers

laughing and running his hands through his black hair. He was shirtless and passing out mojitos.

I stood there gawking like a wide-eyed child at the mercies of his relaxed, deep-set, brown eyes. He waved at me. I looked away and continued biking. "Wait, come back, ginger snap!" he called out. I stopped my bike.

Ted's family was the wealthiest in town, "they monopolized and damned us all," my mother's ex-boyfriend once said. But Ted wasn't just born into it, he acquired his own wealth when he founded a food delivery app. He had recently sold it, following the death of his late wife.

You read that right.

Ted Yoshida, at only 26 years old, was left a widower by Diamond Alworth. Suicide.

"Don't call me that," I snapped.

"I meant it as a compliment," he said, still catching his breath. "What's your name?" he asked.

"Well, I didn't take it as a compliment." I placed my feet back on the petals.

"I'm sorry! Really, I won't call you that again. Why don't you come have a drink with us?" he offered. I looked back and forth between his face and the boat. He broke into a troublesome grin. "C'mon!" he gestured toward the dock.

I hopped off my bike and he took my hand, leading me onto the yacht. As we boarded, he handed me a drink.

"I'm Ted Yoshida, by the way," he said, ignoring the teasing cheers from his friends.

Tongues of Flowers

"I'm Alba," I replied.

"Alba?"

"Alba Anderson."

"It's a pleasure to meet you, Alba Anderson," he said.

CHAPTER TWO

The Beginning and the End

Frankly, Mr. Shankly by The Smiths

Ted had not been working since he sold his company after Diamond died. He said he was "figuring out his next step." I dodged calls from the restaurant I waited tables at and stepped into his world the few weeks preceding our first meeting. It was a welcomed escape from working doubles at the pub and coming home to crash on the couch of my mom's sleazy boyfriend.

Ted paid for everything, even giving me double the wage I would have earned waiting tables. Most of our time was spent attending film festivals and conventions. We met actors and bought merchandise, he got us hotel rooms though we hardly needed them, we were busy indulging in the after-parties.

"I have decided to pursue film," Ted said. We were picking at some Chinese food in a hotel room in Charlotte after attending a black & white screening.

Tongues of Flowers

"That's exciting, jeez, well don't be shy with the details. Or is it a secret?"

"No secrets." He stroked my cheek with the back of his hand. "Chad and I are going to make a horror film," he said. I had met Chad a couple of times at the festivals. He was exactly what you would imagine someone named Chad to be like.

"That's brilliant, Ted. Seriously, that's amazing. What's step one?" I asked.

"Well, I want to move to probably downtown Raleigh, where Chad lives... it's about to grow like crazy because of some new tax incentives. And you know I don't get along with my family, so nothing is keeping me in Hampstead anymore," he explained.

I didn't know why he fell out with his family; it was a touchy subject for him.

"I understand," I said, trying to hide my disappointment that he was leaving.

But then he said, "I want you to come with me."

"What?!"

"And there's something else," he said. He pulled out a dazzling, opal ring, and slid it to my end of the table like he was selling me something illicit.

I gasped, closing the box. "Please tell me that's not what I think it is," I whispered. He reopened the box. "I've known you for two months, Ted," I said.

"But you love me, Alba. I can tell. We don't have to rush into it I just thought it might give you more incentive to come with me," he said, cupping his hands over mine.

Tongues of Flowers

"Well then clearly you don't know me very well," I said, my tone switching from rageful to contemplative as our eyes met.

"I just really want you, is that enough?" he whispered into my ear, his hands still cupped around my face.

"What about what I want?" I asked, turning my face so he was looking into my eyes again.

"I know you love me, you can't convince me other," he said. I broke into a smile. "See?" He kissed my cheek.

"I do love you," I admitted. I let out a loud exhale and stared at the ring. "So, I suppose it wouldn't make much sense for me to say no, would it?"

He placed the ring on my finger. "I'm afraid not," he said.

And just a couple of short weeks after that, we were on the road to Raleigh.

CHAPTER THREE

The Raleigh Estate

As It Was by Harry Styles

Ted squeezed my hand as we pulled into the driveway of our new home.

The house was absurd.

I wondered how I had gone from living on a couch with holes in it to a mansion in the city with 9 bathrooms. "This seems like a bit much for just the two of us, don't you think?" I asked as Ted put the car into park.

"You haven't even seen the best part!" We walked into the house; everything was white. White walls, white marble floors, white counters, each room had a silver chandelier that must have cost more than I had made in a year of waiting tables.

He led me to the backyard. It looked partly like a concert venue. The "porch" if you could even call it that, was light wood with white pillars, and there was a bar-b-q pit, a hot tub, and a pool.

"This will be great for hosting work parties," he said.

Tongues of Flowers

"I'm not sure how good a host I'd be, I can't cook," I admitted.

He chuckled. "Obviously I'm hiring a cook."

I followed him inside. "We have plenty of bedrooms, this one here could be your office, not sure what you would use an office for though. Maybe you could just do your makeup in here or something," he said.

"I'll put my books in here, do some reading. Maybe I'll even try my hand at writing again, it's been a while," I said.

"I don't think you have quite enough books for a library, let me know if you want some of mine to make it look fuller," he offered.

I didn't have a lot of books because I didn't have a lot of money, at least not before Ted. I grew up at the mercies of the Hampstead Public Library. Ted had many books, though I had never seen him read or even talk about a single one of them.

Our conversation was interrupted by the sound of the front door swinging open. "Hello? Anyone home?" It was Ted's best friend turned film partner, Chad Moore. We headed downstairs.

"Quaint little place you got here." He smirked, punching Ted in the arm.

"Yeah, man, well…"

Chad insisted we join him for dinner at a nearby Italian restaurant. We agreed.

After a grueling 2 hours of business talk, we finally left. Why do rich people take so long to eat?

On our way out I noticed a bookstore with a help needed sign. Nia's Books.

"Have you been to this bookstore, Chad? Nia's Books?" I asked.

Tongues of Flowers

"Uh, let's see." Chad put his hands on his hips and looked the brick building up and down in a way only a man who had drunk a couple glasses of wine would. "Yeah, yeah, maybe, I think so! Yeah, you like to read, Alba?" he asked, looking me up and down.

"Yeah, I do," I replied.

"We were just talking about getting you more books, you should go check it out tomorrow. Enjoy yourself," Ted said.

"I think I'd like to work there actually; they're hiring. I volunteered at the library for a bit in Hampstead, so maybe they'd hire me," I said.

"You don't have to work, you know I got you."

"I know I don't have to, and I do appreciate you for that, but I want to make some of my own friends, and I've always wanted to work at a bookstore," I explained.

"Don't worry man, I'm sure it's all women working there. Nia's Books," Chad whispered to Ted as we walked to our separate cars. I didn't process the comment until I got in the car, so Chad was spared a snarky response.

"Are you sure you want to do that?" Ted asked, once he and I were alone in the car.

"Yes, I've worked my entire life, I think I can manage a part-time bookstore job. Why not? What would you have me do at the house when we have housekeepers most days?" I asked.

"Learn to cook," he mumbled, referencing our earlier conversation.

"I can do both," I said, rolling my eyes. "Or I was thinking maybe I could come work with you on the movie, I could help with the writing," I said.

Tongues of Flowers

Ted furrowed his brows and chuckled. "Babe, what? What do you–why would you do that?" he asked. I felt the heat rush to my cheeks.

"I like reading, and I journal a lot and did well on writing assignments in school, I know I'm by no means a professional, but I could assist whatever writers you hire, and I'll do it for free." I watched him closely as he stared at the road with a puzzled look on his face. "Is there something wrong with me asking that?" I finally asked.

"This isn't some film camp student movie, Alba. This is a serious film; can you please treat it like one?" Ted asked with a frown.

"Ted, I know it's a serious film. I don't mean to offend you, but is it so offensive and absurd of me to ask if I can be an assistant to your writers? Just coffee runs or something?" I asked, tapping into my chest voice, trying to conceal my embarrassment.

"You don't have any film experience," Ted said.

Neither do you. "This could be a chance for me to learn about screenwriting and again I'd work and make myself useful," I insisted.

"You don't even have your GED, Alba! For f'ks sake! Get your life in order before taking over mine," he fumed, at a volume I'd never heard him use before, his hands going pale from clutching the steering wheel.

I was silent for the rest of the car ride.

CHAPTER FOUR

How Was I to Know

Dreams by The Cranberries

Nia's Books was just a 20-minute walk from our new home. I passed several massive historical homes and wondered about the people who lived there. I walked by a church and wondered about the people who prayed there. I had never been the religious type, but the tall, white chapel was beautiful.

The bookstore was in a small, brick building. I entered through the glass doors and was greeted by a woman who looked to be in her thirties. "Hello! What are we reading today?" she asked, cheerfully. She was dressed in an array of bright colors and had pink butterfly clips in her afro. Her glasses made her eyes large; she looked like a cartoon character. She was incredibly cute.

"Hi, my name is Alba. I saw you guys were hiring, I just moved here and would love to give you my resume," I said, handing her the document. She held the paper close to her face.

"Hmm, you used to work at the library?" she asked.

Tongues of Flowers

"I was a volunteer, yeah. Back at Hampstead," I said.

"That's by the beach, right?" she asked. I nodded.

"Why did you move?" She peered up at me from her glasses.

"My fiancé wanted to move here for his job."

"What's his job?"

"He's a filmmaker," I replied.

She raised her eyebrows. She looked me up and down and then stared at me for a long moment. I fiddled with my fingers and smiled awkwardly. "Hmph. When can you start, Alba?" she asked.

"Anytime, as soon as possible, preferably." I let out a sigh of relief.

She chuckled. "How does tomorrow morning at 10 sound?"

"That sounds great, thank you, uh, sorry, I didn't get your name," I said.

"Sorry about that! My name is Nia, if you forget it's in big letters in front of the store, and it'll be the name signing your paycheck," Nia said with a wink.

"I probably should have put that together," I admitted, though Nia looked very young to own a bookstore.

"And that's Skipper, behind you," she said.

I turned around to see a young man sitting on the floor with bleached-white hair and umber skin covered in green tattoos. He stood up, revealing that he had a large build, his hand swallowed mine as he shook it.

"Are we the only employees?" I asked.

Tongues of Flowers

"Nah. There are two others, a Bible thumper and a raging lesbian," Skipper said with a half smirk and dazed eyes. Nia whacked the back of Skipper's head. "What? It's true!" he exclaimed.

"And Skipper, here, lives in his mom's basement," Nia said, looking at me with her thumb pointed to Skipper.

"'Hey! It's both pleasant AND fiscally responsible!" Skipper insisted. They both laughed and bantered in a way only close friends would.

I stayed for a few more minutes before heading home. I found out Skipper was the tech-savvy member of the group, and that I would meet the "Bible thumper and raging lesbian," the next day.

As I walked home, I daydreamed about the stories I might tell if I could ever make it to the writer's room. Ted could have helped me with that, so easily. I considered bringing it up again, but it was not worth it if he was going to snap at me again. I would have to find my own way.

Erin, our housekeeper, had already left for the day by the time I got back. I poured myself a glass of strawberry lemonade and swam in the privacy of our backyard pool, the pinnacle of luxury. I looked at my reflection in the pool water, a strong contrast between my dark skin and ginger hair, my hair was a painful reminder of my brother.

My brother, Loo, also has red hair. Mom didn't keep in touch with Loo's dad either. She was 90% certain it was a military guy. Loo himself ended up leaving me to join the Marines. The last time I had heard from him he was stationed in the North Pole, Alaska. We didn't speak much. But I missed him terribly, or at least the version of him I knew as a child.

After my swim, I showered and changed into a black romper. I cooked one of the few dishes I knew how to make, chicken alfredo.

Tongues of Flowers

I set out two plates, but hours passed, and Ted hadn't come home. I texted him asking when he would be back. No reply. I watched a movie and ate a bowl of pasta. Still no reply. It was midnight.

I tried to sleep, but I could not help but worry something happened to Ted. I called. Several times.

He finally stumbled into the room drunk at 4 am.

"What the hell, Ted? Where were you?" I asked.

"I was," he let out a long, slow exhale, "uh, working."

"Why didn't you answer the phone? I was worried something happened," I asked.

He scrunched his nose and side-eyed me like I was a stranger harassing him. "I didn't check my phone, I figured you were sleeping," he finally said.

"Ted, please answer next time, I work at 9 in the morning tomorrow and I'm going to have to go in with zero sleep because I have been up worrying about you for hours," I said, turning my body to face him in the bed.

He yelled out a swear. "I'm not resp—it's not on me what YOU do! It's not! IT'S NOT," he cried as he kicked the bed and shook his head religiously.

"Ted, stop! I didn't say that!" I begged. Before I could say anything else he got on top of me and bellowed like an animal.

"IT'S NOT ON ME WHATEVER YOU F'KIN' DO, YOU CHILD," he screamed into my face, a combination of sweat and spit trickled from his face onto mine, his breath smelled like gin.

"What is wrong with you!?" I cried. We had drunken together before, I was certainly no saint myself, but this time he was different.

Tongues of Flowers

Nothing like himself, I thought, but in hindsight, maybe that was the closest to his actual self I had been.

He clenched a chunk of my hair in each hand. He held the strands so tightly his hands quivered, but he didn't pull. We were both silent for a moment. He finally got off me and ran to the bathroom. I rolled over and put the blankets over me. I pretended to be asleep when he came back out. He crashed as soon as his head hit the pillow. The birds had already started chirping by the time I fell asleep.

I woke up to Ted gently rubbing my arm. He wore a white button-up shirt, and his hair was wet from his shower. He smelled like his cologne, which I loved the smell of. Any evidence of vomit was gone. He looked pretty, not like the drunken devil I had encountered the night before.

"I'm sorry about last night, I drank way too much. I'm sorry," he said in a soft tone as he stroked my cheek.

"You were awful," I said, my voice cracking. I sounded so small. I hated that.

"I know, babe. I'm sorry, it won't happen again." He stared at me, and I stared at our dresser behind him for a long moment, just to avoid his gaze. "I got you a muffin and a latte from the bakery across the street," he said, handing me the cup. I sat up and took a sip.

He rubbed my back. "Do you forgive me?" he asked, pushing my hair behind my ears.

"I mean, I guess, Ted. You're my fiancé," I said.

"I love you so much, Alba," he said, resting his head on my lap as I had my breakfast. His skin was so clear, like a doll.

Tongues of Flowers

"I love you too, Ted," I replied.

CHAPTER FIVE

The Seminarian

First Day of My Life by Bright Eyes

As I walked to my first shift at Nia's Books, I noticed a gray, rain cloud following me there. I tried to outrun it, but it began to pour as soon as I hit the parking lot.

A young man was walking into the bookstore with an umbrella, just as he was about to walk in, he looked back and noticed me. He ran over to me and put the umbrella over my head.

"Hi!" he said. His skin was bronze, and his nose and cheeks were flushed. He had this big, brilliant smile. His hair was black and wavy. He wore a green sweatshirt, which complimented his soulful, dark eyes. He was handsome, and I noticed right away that he exuded an inexplicable warmth.

"Hi, thanks," I said.

"You have a name tag, but I've never seen you before," he said. He was one of those people who smiled as they spoke, in a terribly charming manner.

Tongues of Flowers

"It's my first day," I muttered. He opened the door for me.

"Well, that's great, so your name's Alba?" he asked. I nodded.

"Well, I'm Eleo, and that's Donnie over there," he said, pointing to the woman at the counter. She was short and curvy with pink hair. She had all sorts of tattoos, piercings, and glitter covering her brown skin. She gave me a salute. She looked like a pixie.

"So, this is the Bible thumper and raging lesbian, I presume?" I asked, looking at Nia, who was also behind the counter.

Eleo and Donnie both busted into laughter. "That's how you described us?" Donnie asked, looking at Nia.

Nia shook her head, "that one's on Skipper, not me," she said.

"I mean he wasn't wrong," Donnie said under her breath, elbowing Eleo, who let out a chuckle.

"Okay, well, anyway, I have to head out for a few hours, but you're in good hands with these two. I'll have Donnie train you on shelving today, and then Eleo can train you on register tomorrow," Nia said. I noticed a golden cross around Nia's neck as she tossed her backpack over her shoulders.

Donnie led me to the mystery section to shelve a cart of books.

Spine.

Spine.

Spine.

Face out.

Spine.

Spine.

Spine.

Tongues of Flowers

Face out.

Spine.

Spine...

"So, Nia told me your fiancé is a filmmaker? What films has he made?" Donnie asked, looking up at me with her twinkling brown eyes.

"He's working on his first, he's producing it. He created Food4U and sold the app, so he has money from that," I said.

"He CREATED Food4U?" she asked, setting down her pile of books and staring at me wide-eyed.

"Crazy stuff, right?" I had grown accustomed to the big reactions.

"You guys must be loaded," Donnie said, returning to her work.

"He is," I agreed.

"Well, you're his fiancé, doesn't he share?" she asked.

"Yeah, he does share," I admitted. "What about you? Are you seeing anyone?" I raised my eyebrows.

"Always." She winked. "But nah, I'm more focused on my music right now, I'm a vocalist for a band," she said.

"Yeah? Tell me about it."

"So, we're currently called Widow's Knee," Donnie paused, "pretty cool, right?" she asked.

"Oh, yeah, absolutely," I said.

"You should come see us sometime."

"I will, let me know your next show."

Tongues of Flowers

"Eleo does music too!" she said, loud enough that Eleo could hear from the front of the store.

"She doesn't want to hear about that," Eleo yelled back to us. He was carrying a stack of books, and the sun was shining behind him through the glass windows. I looked probably a moment too long.

"A bit of a different tempo though," Donnie said, looking at me. "He writes that acoustic-Christian-emo-boy shi–"

He cackled from the front of the store. "Is that what you'd call it?" he said before meeting a customer at the register.

"So what's his deal?" I whispered to Donnie.

"Who? Eleo?" she asked.

"Yeah."

"Well, he's cool, he's a good friend. He goes to the seminary nearby and has an apartment there," she said.

"His parents live around here too?" I asked.

"Died in a car wreck when he was a kid, actually," she replied.

"That's terrible," I said. "So, he's going to be a pastor or something?"

"Yeah, I guess, I don't know, something like that. He's a music intern at a church right by here,"

There were some preachers back in Hampstead, they didn't look like Eleo.

"Is it the chapel on Main Street?" I asked.

"Yeah! That's the one. Hey, take these to the counter, they're not scanning right. Nia will have to look at them when she gets back," Donnie said, handing me a stack of small, mass-market novels.

I walked towards the front with my book stack. I mindlessly scanned the front of the and tripped over a small cart of books.

"Are you okay?" Eleo ran over and kneeled to my level. He smelled incredible. Orange blossom? Basil? Ginger?

"Do you have plants?" I blurted out.

His look of concern softened, and he smiled. "I do," he said. "Are you okay?" he asked, containing a laugh.

"Yeah, yeah, I'm fine," I said, looking around at the mess I had made.

He extended his hand. His hand was large and a bit calloused on the tips of his fingers, but I placed my hand in his, and his touch was so gentle. He placed his other hand on the small of my back as he helped me up.

"Don't feel bad, we've all done it!" Donnie called out from the back.

Eleo nodded in agreement, looking at Donnie and then back at me. "It's true," he admitted, his hand sliding away from my waist.

We looked at each other for a moment, and I felt a chill run down my spine. I broke our gaze by clearing my throat and leaning over to pick up the books, Eleo quickly followed suit.

CHAPTER SIX

Take it Like a Woman

Lucky One (Taylor's Version) by Taylor Swift

"I have a surprise for you!" Ted exclaimed as I walked into the living room and set my purse on the counter.

"Oh?"

"Look." He pulled a black cocktail dress out of a silver bag from a store I had never heard of, and the price tag gave away why. "I'm taking you to a party tonight! It's a work thing really, Jonabee Isaac, the director, you know, it's his party. So, a great networking opportunity," he said, tossing me the dress.

"Jonabee Isaac? Seriously? He has a place in Raleigh?" I asked.

Ted kissed my head. "Everyone has a place in Raleigh these days, babe."

We pulled into a circular driveway. The house was almost as large as ours. There was already quite a crowd there. I held onto Ted's arm as we walked up to the house. I imagined how out of place I would have felt if Ted were not with me. Even with my supposed walking security blanket next to me, I had that sick, anxious feeling in the pit of my stomach.

As soon as we walked in Ted began bouncing around the room, socializing at a pace I could not keep up with. I eventually lost track of him and found myself backed against the wall with a gin and tonic in my hand, the smell reminded me of the other night, when Ted climbed on top of me and screamed like an animal. I couldn't bring myself to drink it. I clasped my black nails tightly against the clear glass.

"That can't be your natural hair color," Chad said, appearing out of nowhere.

"It is," I reckoned.

"Aren't you Puerto Rican or something? Your skin is too dark, there's no way," he said, grabbing a strand of my hair.

I slapped his hand away. "I'm half Mexican, and we come in all different colors and shades," I snapped, turning my body away from him.

"Do the curtains match the drapes?" he asked.

I mumbled a stream of profane words and walked away to find Ted.

"I was kidding, come back!" Chad called out.

I eventually found Ted. He was alone with a tall, thin blonde who had an ethereal face that seemed familiar. She was sitting on the pool table, and he was leaning against it, next to her.

"Am I interrupting something?" I asked, folding my arms.

Ted took a step back from the woman and froze for a moment. "Alba! Come here, meet Yana," he finally said.

Tongues of Flowers

"I thought you looked familiar, you're on that werewolf show on the CU, right?" I asked.

Ted and Yana both looked at each other and laughed.

"Alba… she's been in a lot of other projects since then…"

"Oh, sorry?" I said.

Yana placed her hands on Ted's shoulder. "Don't worry about it," she said looking at me for just a moment, and then giving Ted a wink and hopping off the pool table. She walked out of the room.

"Did you need something?" Ted asked.

"Chad was being a jerk," I said. "I was uncomfortable, so I came to find you."

"What did he do?"

I explained to him what had happened. He led me out of the room and found Chad.

"Why were you talking to Alba like that, man?" Ted asked, his face inches away from Chad's. Chad broke into a grin and pushed on Ted's shoulder gently.

"C'mon man, you know how I talk, she didn't think I was hitting on her did she?" he asked. "It's like at the restaurant dude, she doesn't get our humor," he shifted his attention towards me.

"Look, Alba, I'm sorry, I didn't mean anything by it, just ignore me when I've had too many of these," he said, raising his beer. That seemed to be adequate for Ted, who laughed off the ordeal and continued to socialize, I found a space on the couch and observed Yana and Ted's glances at each other until it was time to leave.

"What were you and Yana doing when I walked in?" I asked as I buckled my seat belt.

Tongues of Flowers

"Why?" Ted asked.

"It was just kind of weird you guys were all alone and close together, and then eye screwing the rest of the night," I said.

Ted's face fell. He stopped the car. "Get out," he said.

"Ted, stop! Drive the car! We're in the middle of the road!" I yelled. He didn't budge so I got out of the car and began walking in the direction of the house. He eventually circled back around and gestured for me to get in the car.

I got in and he was dead silent until we pulled into the driveway. Before exiting the car, he screamed the F-word and punched the Bluetooth screen, so hard that it shattered. I did not say anything, I tried to conceal the look of horror on my face, thinking how much more that might provoke him.

As soon as we got to the house I went straight to the bathroom and the tears immediately streamed down my cheeks. In the mirror was an image I resented, the same tears I watched fall from my mother's cheeks as I peeked through the cracks of the closet door as a child. The same fear that made her stay when we ought to have run. The only difference was that I was dressed up in name brands. I thought things were going to be different, but they were instead starting to feel very familiar.

I decided it was enough that he had chosen me and was providing for me. And it still wasn't worse than my situation in Hampstead.

"Everyone fights, Alba, don't be so dramatic," my mother once said, when I confronted her the morning after her boyfriend gave her a black eye by beating her with his shoe.

CHAPTER SEVEN

Tongues of Flowers

Mystery of Love by Sufjan Stevens

I walked into the bookstore, reluctantly. I had been down for days and was strongly considering quitting. I wore sweats because I was behind on laundry, and I could feel a small knot forming underneath my hair. A perfect reflection of how I felt. I did not want to be seen, I would have much rather barricaded myself in my room with a pile of books, just to pretend I was anyone but myself.

Eleo was supposed to be training me that day. I found him sitting on the floor with a group of children around him. "What is he doing?" I asked Skipper, who was leaning against the register.

"Storytime, we do it every Saturday," he said. "Is he supposed to be training you today?" Skipped asked.

"Yes."

"He should be done soon, just hang tight," Skipper said, patting my shoulder, his clanky black and silver jewelry fell to the ends of his wrist as he did so.

Tongues of Flowers

I perused through the aisles and found myself at the children's shelves, next to where Eleo was hosting the children's event. I peeked my head over to get a glimpse. He was telling them a fantasy story, strumming his guitar for dramatic effect.

"Then she entrapped the snake into vines of ivy. She ran out of the Room of Jewels as fast as she possibly could. She never looked back, and she took only the emerald pendant, which led her to a home she didn't even realize she had," he said. The children cheered as Eleo chronicled the protagonist's fortunate fate.

As the story ended Eleo stood up, I walked deeper into the aisles and acted like I was not listening. "Have you heard that story before?" he asked, leaning against the shelf. His lips reminded me of the pink orchids I had seen outside the chapel.

"No," I said abruptly. I turned around and walking toward the cash register. "So how do I do this?" I asked, avoiding his gaze. I suppose coldness is a childish disguise for attraction, but it was the best I could come up with.

Eleo leaned beside me and told me where to click. "Put your employee number there to log in," he said. When he leaned over to point at the screen his chest gently brushed my arm. His breath smelled so fresh.

Eleo was personable with the customers, in a way I could never imitate. He was kind, and he found a way to relate to everyone. I wondered how he managed to find a talking point for every book of every genre.

"Are you okay?" he asked, perhaps I was wearing my dreadful mood on my face.

"Yes, why?"

Tongues of Flowers

He gently smiled at the ground, considering his next words. "Moving sucks, and you don't have any family here, do you? That must be hard," he sympathized.

"No, I don't. My brother is with the Marines in Alaska and my mother lives by the beach. I'm not close to either of them, at least not anymore," I said, stopping rather abruptly as I realized I was oversharing. "What about you? Donnie told me about your parents, I'm sorry," I said.

"Oh, well thank you, there's no need to apologize though. I count myself fortunate to have grandparents here in North Carolina, and another grandparent in Mexico who calls just about every night, I'm thankful for them. The Lord was kind in that way. You must feel that way about your fiancé," he said.

"Yeah," I said, my eyes shifting to the counter. I changed the subject. "Will I ever meet tus abuelos?" I asked.

His eyes perked. "You speak Spanish!?" he exclaimed.

"Poquito," I replied. "My dad was Mexican, or I guess is still Mexican, I don't know his name and he doesn't know I exist as far as I know, so, yeah, I don't know," I said, mumbling at the end.

"Your mother won't tell you his name?" Eleo asked.

"She would tell me if she knew it, I think," I replied.

"Oh, I see, how do you feel about that?" he asked.

I clenched my jaw and shot him a look of distrust.

"Sorry, I don't mean to be intrusive. You've just had such an interesting life! And you're fun to talk to," he said.

"Fun to talk to? We've hardly spoken," I said.

"You're not having fun?" he teased from across the counter.

Tongues of Flowers

Before I could answer we were interrupted by a customer. She was looking for some farmer's almanacs, and as we led her to the section, my eye caught a rusty, old flower reference book. After the customer left, I began skimming the book.

"I have that book!" Eleo beamed.

"What is it exactly?" I asked.

"Well, as members of posh society, there were certain sentiments Victorians could not express forthrightly, so instead they assigned secret meanings to flowers, to say what they could not," he explained. He met my curious eyes with a spirited grin, as if he were imparting to me a clandestine language of our own making.

"And so, this book is like a dictionary for the tongues of flowers?" I asked.

"Yes, if you want to put it so eloquently," he teased.

I traced my fingers over the dilapidating spine of the old reference book. "I think I'll buy it."

CHAPTER EIGHT

The Mischief of Isolation

Innuendo and Out the Other by Cave In

Ted picked me up from work. "Hi doll," he said, leaning over and kissing my cheek. "Let's get dinner, anywhere you want, what are you feeling?" he asked. We eventually agreed on Italian.

I watched Ted as he watched his menu. His hair was slicked back how I liked it. The sleeves of his red shirt were rolled up, exposing his Jaeger-LeCoultre watch. The waitress was dazzled, she called him baby right in front of me and Ted thought it was the funniest thing.

"I'm leaving tonight. My flight leaves around midnight, I have some appointments in Atlanta the next couple of days, I'll be back midweek and then I'll be at the beach for a bit during the weekend, we're getting some drone footage there," he explained.

"I could probably get off the weekend, we could go together," I suggested.

"Yeah, I actually wanted to talk to you about that," he said.

Tongues of Flowers

I sighed. "Yes?"

"I don't think you can handle being around my work stuff, you get too paranoid and it's too much for you," he said.

"Are you joking?" I asked, setting down my fork.

He grimaced. "No?"

"All because I asked what you and Yana were doing?"

"Babe, these are professional relationships, I can't have people who work for me feeling uncomfortable," he said.

"I didn't even ask about it in front of her though, why would she have felt uncomfortable?" I asked, crossing my arms.

"Well, there was also the thing with Chad."

"He was being inappropriate."

"Calm down, Alba! Think about it, what's the common denominator in both of those situations?" he asked.

I shook my head and leaned back in my seat. "I don't want to go anyway."

Once we got home, I took out my GED study book and Ted left for the airport.

My brother called me in the early afternoon.

Me: Hi Loo.

Loo: Please tell me it's not true.

Me: What?

Loo: That you're engaged to Ted Yoshida? And living with him?

Me: I am.

Tongues of Flowers

Loo: Alba, you need to get out of there. I've been hearing stuff about him.

Me: What stuff?

Loo: That he's the reason his wife killed herself. He acted weird after she died. Maybe he killed her.

Me: What are you insinuating? Don't be ridiculous, she threw herself off a bridge! There was a security camera, Loo. And of course, he started acting strange, his wife killed herself. That's traumatic. Cut him some slack.

Loo: Please, Alba. If you don't want to go back with mom I'll fly you out to Alaska, it's beautiful out here!

Me: What would I do in Alaska, Loo?

Loo: You could stay with me; I just got an apartment.

Me: You're not in the barracks anymore?

Loo: No, I got promoted and was able to move off base.

I considered it for a moment. If Loo wanted me around, he should not have left me alone in that nightmare in the first place. Ted wanted me around, and he cared more for me than Loo or my mother ever had.

Me: I don't want to leave. I'm happy here.

Loo groaned and we switched the subject.

That evening I packed up a couple of books and headed to a diner downtown. As I was heading in, I noticed a group of people outside what looked like a food pantry or a shelter. Amidst the group was Eleo. He was sitting with a homeless man who had messy blonde hair and sad eyes. On the other side of Eleo was a pretty woman, she

Tongues of Flowers

was wearing a short skirt, she had blue eyes and honey-colored hair, and wore posh jewelry.

She looked exactly like the type of person I would have pictured for Eleo.

Eleo looked over at me. Our eyes met as I opened the door to the diner, he waved at me, and I nodded back. I settled into the booth and skimmed through my compilation of romantic poems. It was a Mexican diner, but to the amusement of my waiter, I ordered a Gringo Platter.

Just as I was getting ready to leave Eleo busted through the doors. His eyes scanned the restaurant until they fell upon me. "You're still here!" he exclaimed with a ridiculous grin. The host raised an eyebrow at him. "Sorry!" he mouthed.

He walked to my table; I stood up. "I was just leaving," I said.

"Oh. Do you want a ride home?" he asked.

"No. I already called a driver, but thanks anyway." I walked around him and out the door. He followed me out.

"You can cancel it, save your money!"

"No."

"Okay." He paused. "Here," he said, handing me a white acacia.

"Where did you get this?" I asked, holding the delicate flower in my hands. The Taxi pulled up. My cheeks caught on fire.

"There's a flower shop just around the corner," he said.

"Uh..." I opened the door to the taxi.

"Check the book!" he called out.

I shut the door to the Taxi.

Tongues of Flowers

As soon as I got home, I opened my flower reference book.

White Acacia- "friendship"

CHAPTER NINE

Without Pretension

The Lakes (Original Version) by Taylor Swift

The next day I was working with Eleo and Skipper. I stopped at the flower shop before my shift and got a "Flora Bell." The reference book said Flora Bells were code for "without pretension" which seemed like a fitting response to Eleo's gesture of friendship.

I placed the flower in front of Eleo without saying a word. He laughed like a child and grabbed one of the reference books off the shelf. He paced around the store flipping through the pages until he found it.

"Without pretension?" he finally asked.

"Without pretension," I confirmed.

"Care to elaborate?" he probed, tilting his head.

"Doesn't that defeat the purpose?" I teased.

He smiled and raised his arms in defeat. "Without pretension!" he declared as he walked towards the back of the store.

Tongues of Flowers

I helped Skipper and Eleo set up some tables. "What are these for?" I asked.

"Eleo's book club," Skipper replied.

"Has anyone told you about the book clubs?" Eleo asked.

"No," I replied with a tone of intrigue.

"We each get to run a monthly book club here at the store. Nia does biographies. Skipper does fantasy. Donnie does harlequins. I do Christian books," Eleo explained.

"That sounds fun," I admitted.

"What are you going to pick for yours, Alba?" Skipper asked. Eleo watched me as I pondered.

"Hm, I don't know. I like poetry," I said. "So maybe that."

I once again found myself sneaking through the aisles as Eleo engaged with his friends. The girl with the blue eyes was there, among others. She watched Eleo with stars in her eyes, and she could hardly be blamed.

Eleo spoke with such passion, he had an ache in his voice and used grand hand gestures. He loved God. He would die for God. He would go whereever God leads. Why waste such a precious life when you only get one?

I could quite easily bear the thought of those vulgar preachers from Hampstead wasting their lives, but not Eleo. He was too good, too smart, too kind.

"You should join us next time," Eleo said after everyone else had left.

"Why would I do that?" I asked.

Tongues of Flowers

"Well, it might be more engaging than eavesdropping." He nudged me.

"You got me," I admitted, smiling at the ground.

"Are you a follower of Jesus?" he asked.

"No, definitely not. I don't like religion, not my thing," I said adamantly.

"Why is that?"

"Lots of hypocrites and a–holes in my town, I guess," I mumbled.

"I'm sorry, did something happen?" he asked.

I shook my head. "No, just kind of observed from a distance and it doesn't line up with what I want for myself."

"Fair enough." He bit his lip and looked to the ground for a moment before probing further.

"But what if it's the truth?"

"It's not my truth."

"But what if it's the truth? What if Jesus is who He said? Wouldn't your truest life be somewhere in Him?" he asked, bobbing his head back up, with starry eyes.

"Well, I don't know if He is the truth, I don't think anything coming out of these hypocritical Christian's mouths is true, to be honest," I paused, "no offense."

He laughed. "No worries, the Church has had its moments of hypocrisy, myself included, but Jesus isn't like that," Eleo said.

Tongues of Flowers

"I mean, I'm sure there is a God, cosmically speaking, and in terms of human design, there could be. But this isn't for me, never has been. I just see right through it," I explained.

"And what exactly do you see through it?" he asked.

"What do you mean?"

"Well, isn't the idea of seeing through something that you see something through it? What do you see?" he asked.

"Still deciphering," I replied. "But enough about that..."

"Okay," he said softly.

"Was that your girlfriend?" I asked.

"Who?" He was surprised by my question. He blushed and his eyes widened.

"The blue-eyed girl with you at your book club, and she was with you at the diner."

"Oh, no. Pastor's daughter," he said.

"So, you're single?" I asked, taking a step closer to him, mindlessly, but full of heart.

"Yes," he said, just above a whisper, his Adam's apple falling down his throat.

We were standing so close together.

"And you're engaged," he whispered, pointing a finger at me. I took a step back.

"Yeah."

CHAPTER TEN

Truth's Safe Haven

Pretty Woman by Roy Orbison

    "The Boy. The Cat. The Dog."

    You throw me your crumbs

    I want to leap into your lap

    But I have a suspicion

    You'll shake your head and laugh

    saying,

    "Oh, I much prefer cats."

    I ripped up the index card. I wanted to write about anything but Eleo, but he had already pitched his tent in the forefront of my mind, or at least the version of him I had crafted in my imagination had.

    For inspiration, I made my way to Ted's bookshelves to peruse his poetry selection, which was admittedly scarce. His shelves were filled with the works of Vonnegut and Hemmingway.

Tongues of Flowers

I managed to find a slim, red collection of poems by a poet called Melody Evangeline. A crumbled piece of paper fell out of the book. It had 3 handwritten poems on it.

"Dead Eye Boy"

Walking city tavern streets

You're looking at everyone except for me

I wrapped up my life as a gift for you

But now I feel nothing

At least…

Not for you

D.Y.

"Red"

I traced my fingers

Over scarlet letters

You startled me

"You read it before?"

I gasp

you laugh

It bored me

I said

You come up to find me

Something that may be

A little more interesting

D.Y.

Tongues of Flowers

"A Haunting Odor"

Forbidden fruit

Rotting through

Rustic floorboards

Wandering eyes

Sweaty palms

Selfish indulgence

What have we done?

D.Y.

D.Y....

Diamond Yoshida? Ted's late wife?

I wondered if she was writing from personal experience.

Perhaps it is nothing more than bored, housewife-bred fantasies.

Fiction.

Yet does not all fiction ride upon the shoulders of truth?

The front door slammed shut. I closed the red book, shoving Diamond's poems into my pocket. Ted stomped up the stairs, humming the tune of Pretty Woman by Roy Orbison.

"What're you up to?" he asked, poking his head into the room, his eyelids half shut.

He was obviously high, but I didn't remark on it. "Just browsing for inspiration, I think I'm going to start a poetry club," I said.

"A poetry club?!" he asked, with a look of shock that could be explained only by his lack of sobriety.

Tongues of Flowers

"Yeah, at Nia's, every employee gets to run a book club."

"Nice," he whispered, as he walked over to me. He put one hand on the bookshelf and the other around my neck. "I love you," he said, looking straight at me. I tried to convince my eyes to lock with his, but they wanted to look anywhere but at him, it seemed.

"Love you," I mumbled. He kissed my lips, he tasted terrible.

He wrapped his hand around my wrist and led me to the bedroom, with my other hand I clutched the piece of paper, digging it deeper into my pocket.

Ted passed out before much of anything happened.

CHAPTER ELEVEN

O Sacred Truth

Who I Am Hates Who I've Been by Relient K

The next morning, I found myself in a rather awkward predicament. The store hadn't opened yet. Eleo and Nia were at the front counter praying, which should not have been awkward. I thought perhaps I was vain for feeling so strange standing there, just watching.

Eleo's lips were bow-shaped. They looked so gentle and fleshly. And his cheeks looked so soft.

They raised their heads, sealing their prayers with an amen, and then looked over at me.

Later that day, when the business died down, I wandered up to Nia. "So, you're a Christian, right?" I asked.

"I am!" she admitted with wide eyes and a cheerful grin.

"Do you go to the same church as Eleo?"

"Yes, I do," she answered.

Tongues of Flowers

"That white chapel, not far from here, right?" I confirmed.

"Right," she agreed. I nodded and returned to my work. I wasn't sure why I was asking her those things.

I encountered many Christians back in my hometown, and they could all be sorted into two categories.

1. The cliquey country kids who bullied the sensitive kids in gym class.
2. The fire & brimstone preachers who screamed through their megaphones, though they barely needed them. We heard them loud and clear. I think perhaps they were so loud, I could not hear them at all.

But Nia and Eleo weren't like that. They talked about their faith a lot, and at times it irked me, but something about it also drew me in.

I liked Nia a lot. She was fun. Kind.

And I wouldn't admit it aloud, but I liked Eleo. Maybe too much.

"What about you?" Nia asked.

"What about me?"

"What do you believe?" she clarified.

"I don't know. But not Christianity, I don't believe that to be true," I admitted.

"Why not?" she asked.

"I don't like what I know of it," I explained. She nodded politely. "You can tell me what you're thinking, Nia," I added.

"Not liking something doesn't make it untrue, dear."

Tongues of Flowers

"It's not untrue to me in the sense that I don't think there's a sphere where it doesn't exist, maybe it, He, does. I just don't care to exist within that sphere, I want to make my own way," I said.

She smiled warmly.

"Why are you smiling like that?" I asked.

"I have this strange feeling, that you actually are in His 'sphere' you just haven't realized it yet," she said.

I chuckled and returned to my work. "Well, time will tell, won't it, Nia?"

She agreed.

I later found myself conversing with Eleo. He rolled up the sleeves of his dark green sweatshirt. "Have you been thinking about the poetry club at all?" he asked. His dark hair was beginning to curl at the ends a bit.

I told him all about my plans for the poetry club, I felt like a child who was just waiting for someone to ask about their favorite toy, and he listened to me like so.

Attentively. Reacting to every word.

"Do you write at all?" he asked.

"No," I lied, and he grinned like he knew. I blushed. "Do *you* write?" I asked.

"Just what Donnie said, those little songs," he said.

"They're Christian songs?" I asked.

"I mean, I just write about what I'm feeling, I guess I can't help that He seeps through."

I shook my head. "That's so cliché."

Tongues of Flowers

Eleo smiled as he said *He*. He said it like the word was both sacred and safe, everything above him, and the only thing holding his feet to the earth.

I wished I were built for that, for feeling whatever it was that Eleo felt. To know what he knew, or perhaps more accurately, to unknow all that I carried with me.

CHAPTER TWELVE

The Apathetic Mansion on Main St

Freaks by Surf Curse

One evening I was sitting on the couch with Ted, we were eating empanadas from a local joint. He was hyper-focused on his phone, occasionally smiling at his screen, presumably unaware of my stare.

"I think for the poetry club I might encourage people to bring their own poems along with ones they like, like a critique group," I said.

"That's nice, babe."

"Yeah, how's the film going? What stage are you guys at?" I asked.

"It's going good, beginning stages, you know," he said.

He didn't even look up from his phone.

I eventually gave up on trying to have a real conversation with him.

Tongues of Flowers

I took out my phone. I wasn't naturally much of a tech person; I hadn't posted on social media in years. But I opened the old app, and my feed was flooded, mostly with Ted's posts. He had become very active.

There were posts of me, which I liked. Though I quickly realized that wasn't the flex I initially thought it to be. He posted everyone, including Yana. I clicked on her profile.

Most of her posts boasted her tall, lean figure, long blonde hair, and expensive taste. Occasional promotional posters from her films. Quick motion shots captured on a film camera at glamorous parties, most recently, one Ted had also attended.

On the last slide was a photo of Ted's hand on Yana's waist. The photo was taken from behind, but I could tell that it was him. I wanted to question him about it, but what would be the point? For him to throw a tantrum and make me feel sick in the stomach, all for the resolve to be that he was "networking" and that I've gone mad? No thanks.

So, I said nothing.

Even at that moment, I still desperately wanted him to want me. For a moment, I almost thought I might prefer his outbursts to his apathy. But I remembered the smell of gin hitting my face, and the twist in my stomach as I waited for him to pull my hair. I concluded that it was the spell break of his apathy that really made me sick.

Diamond's poetry didn't seem to mention Ted's temper. I wondered if the gruesome temper was a new installment. And did he cheat on her too, or was she easier to love?

I can't say I'm not difficult, after all.

CHAPTER THIRTEEN

Checkmate

The World Is Ugly by My Chemical Romance

The next day I walked into work to find Donnie and Eleo playing checkers on a coffee table near the front. Donnie had dyed her hair blue since her last shift. Eleo's hair fell in his face a bit sometimes, and I wanted to run my fingers through it. I watched him from the cash register as they played their game.

Nia stood next to me while sorting through some paperwork. She side-eyed me and snickered.

"What's so funny?" I asked.

"You should take a picture, it'll last longer." She gave me a wink and gestured towards Eleo and Donnie, I suspected mostly to Eleo.

I scoffed. "I just find their dynamic strange."

"Why?" Nia asked, tilting her head, and turning to face me.

"You holy folk aren't supposed to sit with us sinners," I said, with a sarcastic tone.

Nia chuckled. "You know, there were some religious people back in Jesus' day who thought the same thing."

"Ahh, and what did Jesus think of all that?" I asked.

"He didn't exactly agree with their sentiment," she replied. I said nothing. I shrugged and returned to my work. "I have get going," Nia said, tucking the papers into her bag and pulling out her keys. She waved to Eleo and Donnie. "Oh, and Alba, start with John Chapter 8," she added as she flew out the door.

I pulled a Bible off the shelf. There appeared to be 3 Johns, I figured I should start with the first one. I didn't realize the scriptures were set up in such a strange manner. They could have been a little more creative with the titles.

I came to the verse, though it did not seem related to what Nia was saying.

"Were you looking for John chapter 8?" Eleo said, suddenly standing a foot in front of me.

"Yeah, I'm at the first John but this doesn't seem right," I admitted.

"She might have been referring to the Book of John, not 1 John. They're two different books," he said, as tenderly as possible.

"Oh, I didn't realize…"

"Do you want me to show you?" he asked, taking a step closer to me, I kept the Bible in my hands but turned it to face him. He flipped to the right spot.

"Here it is! John chapter 8." He placed his hands on the bottom of the Bible where my hands were but quickly moved them to his side when our hands touched.

Tongues of Flowers

I began reading. In the story, Jesus was teaching but was interrupted by some folk called the Pharisees, and some others called the Scribes. They had brought to him a woman who had been caught in the act of adultery. Something about those words made my stomach drop.

I had not read the Bible before, but that sounded about right, so far. Buncha' judgementals.

Except, then Jesus said no. He told them to let the one who is without sin throw the first stone, which turned out to be none of them. And then He started writing in the sand. I wondered what He was writing, but it didn't say.

Then he looked at the woman, I could not imagine what she must have been feeling.

He asked her where all her accusers were, and if anyone condemned her.

Before I could read the rest of the story, the shop got busy, and it stayed that way until close.

"Where's Ted? He isn't picking you up today?" Eleo asked.

"No, he's out of town, I'll just walk or catch a Taxi," I said.

"No, no, I'll take you home, c'mon," he said, gesturing to his Sudan.

"I can take you, also!" Donnie chimed in.

"Oh okay, well if you're sure you don't mind, I'll go with you Donnie, thanks," I said.

It took every ounce of self-control to choose Donnie's car and not Eleo's.

Tongues of Flowers

"Before you go, here, so you can finish reading," he said, handing me the same Bible I had been reading out of.

"You bought it… for me?" I asked.

"Uh, well, yeah," he said, letting out a modest laugh. "Is that weird?" he asked.

"No, that's nice, thank you," I said. We looked at each other for a moment. "Goodnight, Eleo."

"Goodnight, Alba."

On the car ride home, Donnie talked about My Chemical Romance and homemade mozzarella sticks. A positive consensus for both, by the way.

"You should give Eleo a chance," Donnie said, rather abruptly.

"What do you mean? We're cool," I said.

"I feel like you're short with him, like you don't like him."

I may have been short with him, but it wasn't because I didn't like him. I wished that had been the issue.

CHAPTER FOURTEEN

The Line You Walked

To Be Alone with You by Sufjan Stevens

    I brought Ted and I's dinner out onto the back patio. I had been trying to practice cooking. I had managed a pad Thai and was quite proud of it.

    "You've learned fast, this's great!" Ted exclaimed.

    "I'm glad you like it," I said.

    We ate silently for a few minutes. "Are you reading The Bible?" he asked, pointing out the brown leather Bible Eleo had given me, which was on the table.

    "Oh, yeah, Nia and one of the guys who work with me, Eleo, well they're both devout Christians, so I don't know, I was curious what it says, I thought I knew, but I don't think I did," I said.

    "I didn't peg you as the religious type," Ted said, grinning a bit.

    I laughed slightly. "As I said, I was just curious about it. What about you? Are you religious?" I asked.

Tongues of Flowers

"Not really, I'm just kind of neutral. My parents were, are, Buddhists, my brother was into that too," he said, his eyes not leaving his plate.

I was surprised by Ted's response. He did not like to talk about his brother, Lee Yoshida. I had never met Lee. I knew he died, but even the internet gave scarce details, I only knew that he had died of an overdose.

Wealth can only get you so far until death suddenly stops discriminating.

We had a pleasant evening until we got into bed. Ted's phone was blowing up.

"Who is that?" I asked, in an unassuming tone.

"Nothing," he said.

Not thinking much of it, perhaps overly comfortable from a relaxing evening with him, I leaned over to his side of the bed and peeked over his shoulder, he slapped me in the face.

I placed my hand on my cheek. He looked at me. "Don't be so dramatic, I was just getting you away from my phone, I didn't hit you," he insisted. I remained still. "STOP!" he whined, more aggressively, removing my hand from my cheek.

I sat back and tried desperately to not react. I maintained the charade until we went to bed, then I snuck off to the hallway bathroom rather than our master, I wanted to be away from him.

He hit me. He slapped me. He just pushed me away. I don't know. What's really the difference? I hate myself. Why am I here? Why does it always come back to this? He was supposed to be my way out. I don't like where this is going. No, he's right, I'm just being dramatic.

Tongues of Flowers

I leaned against the door and slid to the floor. My eyes were too full of tears to see what was ahead of me, and my heart was too full for my mind to sort, so I could only do one thing. Something I had not done before.

I prayed. Simply, but with utmost sincerity. Just 4 words.

Do you hear me?

CHAPTER FIFTEEN

Passing Glimpse

And I Told Them I Invented Times New Roman by Dance Gavin Dance

The next day I passed a busker by the white chapel on my way to work.

He was singing this strange song:

I hear you

O' I have heard you all along

O' I have wanted you all along

Do you feel me somehow?

Do you want to know me now?

I stopped walking. I suddenly wanted to run, I just wasn't quite sure yet to or from what.

I walked into the bookstore pondering the otherworldly.

"Good morning!" Eleo said, chipper as ever.

Tongues of Flowers

"Hey."

"Are you okay?" he asked.

"Yeah, just saw this busker, it was weird," I explained.

"Weird how?"

I laughed. "Nah, it was nothing."

He continued to look at me, urging me to continue.

"This guy by the chapel, it's like he was reading my mind last night," I admitted with an eye roll and chuckle.

"Oh, do you mean Jamal? I think you're giving him too much credit."

My phone buzzed. It was a text from my mother.

Mom: Why haven't you been answering my calls? I need to see you. Please. Come today.

I sighed. Eleo gave me a curious look. "My mom wants me to go see her today, apparently it's important," I explained.

"Are you going to go after work? We're off at noon and she's only a couple of hours away, right?" he asked.

"I can't, Ted's out of town and I don't have a car."

"I'll take you," he volunteered.

"I couldn't ask you to do that," I protested.

"You're not asking, I'm offering, insisting, actually," he said, climbing up the ladder, returning a book to one of the higher shelves. I loved the definition of his shoulder blades as he reached for the top of the shelf. I wanted so badly to trace my fingers over them.

Tongues of Flowers

"Well… thank you."

He just smiled, but it was that cursed half smile that I knew would play in my mind again and again whether I wanted it to or not.

It was five before noon when Skipper and Donnie got to the store to take over for us. I gathered my things and headed for the door. Eleo gently touched the small of my back with one hand and pushed the door open with the other. "Are you ready?" he asked. I looked away and nodded, I didn't want him to see that my face now matched my hair.

He placed his arm behind the back of my seat as he pulled out of the shopping center. I found the most absurdly neutral things about him, wildly attractive. His greenhouse scent, his tethered fingers, and his messy, dark hair. Even the way he drove was attractive to me. And I was to the point where I quite hated his smile and the way it had marked itself in my mind.

At first, we drove without speaking. He had one hand on the steering wheel and the other carefully selecting song after song. He played a lot of country music, but not like beer-and-boobs country, but the kind that had complex narratives and a classic sort of sound. An occasional old pop song. A worship song.

But the real curveball was, And I Told Them I Invented Times New Roman by Dance Gavin Dance. I couldn't help but laugh hysterically.

"What?" he asked.

"Sorry, I just wouldn't have guessed Dance Gavin Dance would be your speed."

"No?" he laughed.

Tongues of Flowers

"Your girlfriend would have a heart attack if she heard this, wouldn't she?" I said, fidgeting with my black skirt.

"My girlfriend?" he asked.

"Yeah, the preppy one with the blue eyes, you know."

"Leah-Jane? I told you, it's not like that," he said. I didn't believe him.

CHAPTER SIXTEEN

Hampstead, NC

Fast Car by Tracy Chapman

It was strange being back in Hampstead. Same big bridge and vast waters. "You miss it?" Eleo asked. I turned to face him.

"Miss what?"

"The water. You're looking at it like you're going to jump out of the car and swan dive in."

"I do miss it. A lot," I admitted.

Eleo told me to call him when I was done with my mother, he saw a sign for a bookstore he wanted to explore.

I was walking into the restaurant when a familiar, nasally voice stopped me, "Ginger snap?"

"Kimberly," I said. She pulled me into a hug, her curly hair tucking itself under my chin.

"Is it true you're livin' with Ted Yoshida now?" she asked, her eyebrows curiously joining together.

Tongues of Flowers

"Yeah, we're in Raleigh."

She placed her hand over her heart. "Whew! Never in a million years would I have guessed you'd end up with Ted Yoshida!" she exclaimed. "Well, anyway, I got to get back to work, I'm glad ya doin' well though," she chirped, pulling her pen out of her apron and scurrying to a nearby table.

Kimberly would never know it, but she had been one of my closest friends. I wasn't even in her top 50. I wasn't very good at making friends or keeping them. Something always went wrong, and I had little grace and little tolerance for much of anything in that area of my life.

I greeted my mother at the table, her hair looked so greasy, and the bags under her eyes so dark.

"You've put on weight," my mother said, with a concerned tone and furrowed brows as she looked me up and down.

"I guess a little," I said, rolling my eyes and sitting down.

"I mean, that ain't all bad, hun. I'm glad he's feedin' you over there, at least."

"Is that why you invited me here? To see if I got fat?" I asked.

"No, no… I think you outta come home, now before you say anything just listen. I talked to your brother, and I've been hearing some people talking at Ken's Bar, something ain't right with that Yoshida boy. He's gone ill," she explained.

"Don't you think I'd know his mental state better than you? Don't I live with him?" I asked, crossing my arms.

"He hurtin' you?" my mother asked, grabbing my arm to check for bruises. I yanked it away.

Tongues of Flowers

"Don't touch me!" I snapped.

"Alba, people say he killed the ex-wife," she whispered in her thick southern accent, leaning forward, and looking around.

"Mom, think, Diamond's suicide was on video. She jumped off a bridge."

"It was night and it was blurry and things aren't always what you think–"

I pulled my chair out. "You're crazy," I said, pointing to her sternly.

"Is he hurtin' you? I'll kill him, Alba, you just tell me," she pleaded.

"No! The only person who's hurt me is you, don't try and act like you care now that I've finally gotten away from you and this awful town!" I cried, running out the door.

I heard my mother apologize to the waitress as the door slammed behind me.

I don't quite know what I was thinking as I sat outside that restaurant waiting for Eleo. Maybe that I wanted to die. Or how angry at myself I was for losing my temper with her when she was trying to help. Or how angry I was that I was now just like her, wasting my life away at the beck and call of someone who didn't love me. Making a fool of myself trying to seduce a decent guy knowing good and well he'll end up with one of the Leah-Jane's of the world.

Just like my momma.

I climbed into Eleo's car.

"That was fast, how did it go?" he asked.

"Awful."

Tongues of Flowers

"Do you want to talk about it?"

"No," I said, turning my knees towards the window.

After a few minutes of silence, he asked, "hey did you ever finish John 8?"

"I got to the part where Jesus stopped them from throwing the stones, and then he was writing on the sand, that's where I left off," I said.

"I have a Bible down there if you want to finish."

I pulled the small, black Bible out from under the seat.

I read the story aloud.

All the people who tried to stone her left, one by one. And then it was just Jesus and the adulteress. I imagined him having a gentle grin as he asked her, "well who's accusing you now?"

She replied, "no one, Lord."

And He said he didn't condemn her either, that she was free to go, sin absolved.

"Easier said than done, I'd say," I said, closing the Bible.

"What do you mean?" Eleo asked.

"My life is so deeply and intricately laced into all that sin is, if I were her, and I were told to return to a life of no more sin, I'd have nothing to return to. It runs too deep," I said.

"There's nowhere so deep that He isn't deeper still."

I sighed and looked toward the window. "You don't think so?" I asked.

"He's saved murderers, adulterers, religious folk, the whole lot. He can save anyone," Eleo insisted.

Tongues of Flowers

Tears streamed down my face. I shoved my fingernails into my skin, angry that I had embarrassed myself like that. I shook my head.

He took one of his hands off the steering wheel and placed it over mine. "Hey! It's okay, it's okay." His thumb stroked my hand. My nails surrendered.

"Are you in a rush to get back?" he asked.

"No," I said, sniffling.

He moved his hand from mine and changed directions. My instincts wanted to pull his hand back, but I let it go. We went over the big bridge that led to the island. He rolled the windows down.

Fast Car by Tracy Chapman was blasting through the stereo. We departed from Hampstead and headed toward Ocean City, onto the bridge where the whole island could be seen. The bridge was so steep it looked like we would just drop off at the end.

I watched him, his lips looked so soft, and they held an unprecedented power over me, whether it be through the kind words in his deep voice or that gut-wrenching smirk.

He pulled into the public beach access.

"You want to go to the beach?" I asked as he jumped out of the car.

He walked around his truck and opened the door for me. "Yeah."

CHAPTER SEVENTEEN

Rays of Gold

Everywhere by Fleetwood Mac

"Did you know we're on top of the Mermaids Chapel?" I asked as we walked along the sandy pier.

"The Mermaid's Chapel?"

"C'mon!" I took his hand and led him to the staircase leading under the pier. I'm not sure why I expected his hand to be limp in mine, it was firm, like he was holding my hand back.

We looked ahead and just like I remembered, the bottom of the pier looked like a mermaid's chapel. The wooden pallets and the sapphire waves told the world's most ancient narrative, not in words, but in feelings.

"I see where you got the name from," Eleo said.

"I can't take credit for that; I think my mother coined the term when I was little."

"Creative," he remarked.

Tongues of Flowers

I sighed. "Yeah, she could be," I admitted.

"But?"

"But she just isn't, I don't know," I said.

Mother was one of those people with so much potential, but who could never seem to make the right decision about anything, ever, completely led by whatever she felt in the moment.

"What about your parents? What were they like?" I asked.

"Oh, they were pretty great, I can't complain," he said. He had every right to complain, yet I had never heard him do so.

"Who are you more like?" I asked.

He looked at me with wide eyes. "Uh…" we stood silently for a moment as he contemplated. "Well, I guess I look like my dad, though he was much smarter than me," he finally said.

"What was your mother like?" I asked.

"Dynamic. Loud. Loving. Generous. Eccentric." He grinned as he listed her attributes.

"She sounds like she was fun," I said.

"Exceptionally so."

Some fishermen started blasting Everywhere by Fleetwood Mac from the top of the pier, the waves complimented it well.

"But I'll tell you this, I'm a much better swimmer than either of them ever could have been," he said, placing his wallet, phone, and keys behind one of the wooden beams.

"What are you doing?" I asked.

He started running toward the water. "You coming?" he called back.

Tongues of Flowers

I quickly tied up my skirt. My sandals flew off my feet as I followed him into the water. Even under the shadow of the pier, the water was warmer than I would have expected for fall. I met Eleo halfway down the pier, I was up to my chest, but he stood there just fine.

We stood face to face, catching our breaths. "How is your hair not wet?" I asked, observing the few drops at the end of his dark waves.

He dunked his face under the water. "Better?" he asked. I nodded, watching the water trickle from his eyes, over his lips, and down his neck. He slicked back his drenched hair.

He interrupted my gawking, "race you," he said, diving towards the end of the mermaid's chapel.

I knew I was a better swimmer, I had to be, I lived on the beach my whole life. I had no friends and no money, so there was never anything to do but swim in the ocean. The only thing Eleo had on me was the element of surprise.

I kicked as quickly as I could, my body felt light, and it was practically gliding on the waves. I quickly passed him. Just as I was reaching the very end of the mermaid's chapel, I felt something grab my ankle and pull me back. I then felt Eleo's hand grab my waist and pull me up, one of his arms was holding onto the wooden beam at the end of the pier.

I instinctually wrapped one of my arms around his neck as I wiped my eyes.

The sun was suddenly illuminating the mermaid's chapel with golden rays. My back was against one of the wooden beams. Eleo still had one arm around my waist, and I still had one of my arms wrapped around his neck.

Tongues of Flowers

I imagined I must have looked like a wide-eyed, wet rat. But he looked so cool. I hated it.

"You cheated," I said, hoping he wouldn't look too closely at me.

"I did," he admitted. "I'm sorry, your ankle was right there, I couldn't resist!"

I shook my head, but we were both laughing. "A fair race this time?" I asked. He agreed.

I dunked his head into the water and kicked off the wooden beam, leaping ahead of him. I heard him laugh from behind me. He couldn't catch up. I won.

I squeezed the water out of my skirt out and he treaded out of the water, his white t-shirt clinging to his body. I looked away.

I felt bad, not so much for wanting Eleo, but for not feeling bad that I wanted Eleo. For wondering if there was potential for a kind of life that I really want, and I was just missing it.

My outlandish fantasies were cut short when Eleo offered to take a picture for some girls trying to take a selfie. They were Leah-Jane sort of girls. They had perfectly neat hair and spray tans, and I knew they would be gushing over how cute Eleo was once we left. And they were right.

It was also a necessary reminder that Eleo was a gentleman, he was polite and kind and a friend to all. I could not let myself fall into the trap of thinking that this was special attention, just because it was special to me.

"Are you ready to head back?" he asked. I was. And we did.

CHAPTER EIGHTEEN

I Would Much Rather Be Wanted than Needed

Heart Like Yours by Willamette Stone

I put my phone on shuffle as I climbed into the shower that evening. I thought about a lot of things.

Mostly, I thought about where my life was going.

Will I work at the bookstore forever?

I like the bookstore.

Will Eleo, Skipper, and Donnie one day move for careers or dreams?

Eventually, Ted will want to move.

Am I just to go with him for the rest of our lives?

What use will he have for me?

He isn't even sleeping with me anymore.

Is this what happened with Diamond?

Tongues of Flowers

He isn't apathetic towards me though; it's just not love.

It's rage.

So, what will he do with me?

Certainly, my purpose in this life can't be to serve as Ted Yoshida's punching bag.

Can it?

I couldn't go back to Hampstead. Living there wasn't living. I didn't want to find one of Mom's boyfriends sitting at the edge of his dirty couch staring me down as I slept. I didn't want to spend the night dodging vases and shoes only for my mother to tell me I don't understand when I beg her to leave the next morning. I didn't want to work doubles 7 days a week and still not be able to afford a place of my own.

I didn't want to be constantly looked down on, like the woman from that story, the adulteress naked on the sand while everyone watched. But nobody was there to stick up for me, nobody to write in the sand so I could clothe myself.

There might be Someone. But I'm afraid of Him.

I was afraid of myself, really, of what He was going to see, of what He had seen all along. A heart, body, and soul full to the brim with rage, much more like Ted than I ever wanted to admit.

Not prim, proper, and beautiful like Leah-Jane. Not gentle and kind like Eleo. Not wise and thoughtful like Nia. But rather someone with an impressive ability to make every wrong choice every time. A perpetually wet cat.

I sunk to the bottom of the shower, tucking my knees into my arms. Heart Like Yours by Willamette Stone was just hitting its chorus. In a dreadfully epiphanic fashion, I shut off the water. I put

Tongues of Flowers

a raincoat over a long plaid dress and tied up my wet hair. I ran outside in my boots, it was drizzling, but I ran into the nearby woods.

It was so dark, but I ran until I couldn't anymore, until I was out of breath and out of earshot.

"God!" I called out, as loud as I could.

"I'm afraid I cannot speak with much sophistication here, not when it comes to You. I have been on the pathway to hell my entire life, but I keep hearing you. How is it that you both enchant and curse me? You must know, I am a fool for it, but I want you and to be yours, but no! Because I already have the expectation that You are laughing at me from heaven right now. This is ridiculous. I'm everything You are not. But You keep calling me, I feel it. I see You in everything. It scares me. I called You once 'cause I thought I wanted You to answer, but now that You have I am afraid. Now, none of this is making any sense, and I keep contradicting myself. But I did warn You I have nothing to offer, no good words or pleasantries or great beauty to lay down here for You. It's just me. And so with that, I just, I wanted you to know I have met my match, here."

I fell to my knees and sat in the silence.

I spoke more quietly this time. In less of a shout into oblivion, and more of a whisper into eternity. "I believe You, now. And I have been told You are willing to forgive me, and even be with me. And I mean, I don't get it, but I need it, I need You, this, whatever this is. For You to have given everything and die on a cross for me is more than I would ever think to ask anyone, even You. But You've already done it, and I have no other hope, no other chance, nothing apart from You. So, I want You, please have me."

CHAPTER NINETEEN

Cameo

Your Best American Girl by Mitski

"You're in a good mood. Is Ted back in town?" Skipper asked.

I smiled as I put up the 20% off sign. "He comes back today, that's not why I'm in a good mood though," I said.

"Well, why are you in a good mood?" he asked, setting up his laptop.

"I don't know. Fresh starts, or something like that."

I found myself in the back of the store, pulling out the Bible. I wasn't sure exactly what I was supposed to read or look for, I just wanted to hear Him. I found myself in the Psalms, chapter 91. It said something about being covered in His feathers, that I could hide in His wings. I couldn't help but smile at the page. I imagined it was largely metaphorical, but I liked the thought of eternity in His wings, safe.

Later that day a familiar face entered the store. Leah-Jane. Her hair was up and she was wearing maroon leggings, and a black t-

Tongues of Flowers

shirt over her perfect figure. Presumably on a jog, though she wasn't sweating, and her hair was perfectly in place.

"Hi! Can I help you find anything?" I asked.

She didn't smile, she simply shook her head and turned to Skipper. "Hey Skippy, is Eleo around?" she asked in a childish tone.

Skipper shook his head. "He's off today. You want me to let him know you stopped by?" he asked.

"Oh, would you?" she beamed. She hugged Skipper from over the counter. "Bye Skippy!" she called back before scurrying out.

Skipper and I made eye contact and immediately fell into a fit of laughter.

"I shouldn't laugh, but what was that!? She completely ignored me! And Skippy?!" I said, still chuckling.

He shrugged, still grinning. "I don't know, that was weird."

"What's going on with her and Eleo, anyway?" I asked.

"Ugh, I don't know. He had said he liked her, but he wasn't sure anything was going to happen. She likes him, she's kind of a flirt though, so I don't know how serious that is," he explained.

"Eleo said he liked her? When?" I asked, my stomach curling.

"Yeah, I mean they grew up together, so it's been a while. But we talked about it a couple of weeks ago," Skipper spoke nonchalantly as he fidgeted with his nose ring. He had no way of knowing that the thought of Eleo with Leah-Jane tormented me.

I had started this strange little habit of praying to God about every little thing, I figured He was with me, so why not?

Tongues of Flowers

God, hi, not sure if it's appropriate for me to ask, but can you just make me not jealous? I can't compete with her, and I don't want to. And I'm engaged. I don't want to feel that.

"What do they talk about? What is she like? I've listened in on Eleo's book club, she didn't seem to have much to say," I said, still bitterly, unfortunately.

"Jeez, I don't know, nothing too interesting, I guess. She's just your stereotypical southern bell, you know, top 40's and cowgirl boots and she's cute, I guess, not my type but attractive," he said.

"I'm sure she's more dynamic than that when you get to know her," an elderly woman who I hadn't even heard enter the store said.

"Yeah, probably. But the guy she's interested in is incredibly dynamic and interesting, he'd be bored to death with her. You aren't suggesting he could be happy with anyone just because they're beautiful and because deep down we're all inherently complex?" I challenged her.

"Are you jealous of her?" the woman asked, suspiciously.

"No!" I insisted.

"I've been around a long time, I'm no fool, sometimes people choose other people for no other reason than vanity, that's how it is," she said. "But if this guy is as spectacular as the stars in your eyes seem to insinuate, then there's either something in her he can see that you don't, or he'll mature and realize beauty is fleeting. Don't worry!" she said, squeezing my arm.

"Worry?! I'm not worried! I'm engaged," I said, scoffing.

"You did sound worried," Skipper mumbled under his breath.

"And jealous," the woman whispered to Skipper, he agreed. I rolled my eyes. Nia was laughing at our conversation from a few

Tongues of Flowers

bookshelves over. "Whatever fire the Lord means to be yours, won't be put out so easily," the woman said, before walking out.

Nia came up to me during my lunch break. "You know he cares about you, right?" she asked.

"Even if he didn't it would be fine."

"Okay." She smiled. "What were you reading earlier?"

"Psalm 91."

"What do you think?" she asked.

"I think all I really want to do lately is hide in His wings," I blurted out. "Jeez, sorry, that was weird. When did I become so corny?" I said, putting my hand over my mouth.

Nia laughed.

CHAPTER TWENTY

The Little Chapel

Without You by RIDERS

When Ted came home, he cupped my face. "I missed you," he said tenderly. "What did you do while I was gone?" he asked.

"I worked, and one of my coworkers took me to see my mom," I said.

"Thank you for doing that while I was gone," he said. He hadn't met her, but my stories didn't paint her in the most flattering light. And though unspoken, we both knew nobody in Hampstead was the biggest Ted Yoshida fan.

"Nia and Eleo invited me to their church," I said, sitting on the edge of the bed, closely gauging his reaction.

"Are you thinking about going?" he asked as he opened his suitcase.

"Yeah, I think so," I said.

Ted laughed. "Are they rubbing off on you, Alba?" he asked.

Tongues of Flowers

"I think they might be," I laughed. "I don't know, I've been talking to God lately, which is super weird, but yeah."

"Whatever makes you happy, babe. I think I would only be concerned if He were talking back," Ted said.

"Well, that's the thing, I feel like He kind of does. Not in the audible way you and I would converse, but in a way that's somehow much truer."

Ted sighed and paused for a moment, ultimately opting to come kiss my head. "Like I said, Alba, whatever makes you happy."

"Sorry, I know it's weird, but do you want to come with me on Sunday?" I asked.

"I'm sorry, it's just a really busy season for me, I don't think I can swing that right now."

"That's okay."

Sunday finally came. I rubbed my sweaty hands on my velvet dress as Nia and I approached the old, white chapel. Eleo stood by the corridor with a group of people about our age, Leah-Jane was of course right next to him.

"You have nothing to be nervous about," Nia said as she put the car in park.

Don't I?

Eleo seemed to sense my presence, seeing that we made eye contact as soon as I got out of the car. He looked so handsome in his green button-up and with his guitar case strapped around his shoulder. It took us a while to get over to him, people kept stopping Nia. She was very popular.

Tongues of Flowers

"I thought you might wimp out," Eleo whispered, leaning close to me as we walked down the aisle with Leah-Jane and Nia.

"Is your dad preaching today?" Nia asked Leah-Jane.

"No, Pastor Reginald, today," she said, straightening her jean skirt. I wondered if I was a bit overdressed.

Pastor Reginald walked onto the stage bright-eyed and bushy-tailed, I couldn't help but notice he looked and sounded eerily like Morgan Freeman. Exactly how a preacher ought to sound if you ask me.

I learned that there was this sermon on this mount, and evidently, Jesus said strange things. It seems everything was backward with Him. Blessed are the poor. The persecuted. Those who mourn.

He certainly did not choose as man would, I had learned.

I could not box Him into any boundary I had ever known.

With Him I could not even expect the unexpected, because I could only ever dream up expectations from a finite line of vision.

He was vast, to say the least.

How can it be that this magnificent Being they're speaking of is You? I know You're here, with me, I really think so, I can't imagine why, but I'll never want You to go.

Eleo suggested I go to lunch with him and his friends since Nia had to stay late for an event. The lunch included Leah-Jane, and a few of their other friends; John, Maisie, and Anne. Everything about them set off both my fight and flight.

They weren't rude, necessarily, but I felt the energy being sucked out of me with all the small talk and pleasantries. I knew how pretentious that sounded too, but I didn't know how to talk about the weather or Maisie's grandma's tractor, I knew that was a fault on my end, though.

I thought about what that old woman had told Skipper and me, that even people who seem "shallow" to me, have more complex and interesting sides, I just hadn't looked hard enough. So, I tried to smile and be pleasant. Again, I knew I was the problem.

"What did you guys think of the sermon?" I asked. They gave me a slight look like they may have heard me but continued on with their conversation about the same summer camp they'd been talking about for the last 35 minutes. Oh, screw what that old lady said, these people are so rude.

But Eleo heard me.

"Well, I'm awfully curious about these heavenly rewards," he said, rubbing his hands together. Though we had become friends, he still made me nervous. He looked at me and his eyes felt like daggers that turn into water the moment they pierced me.

"That's not considered a selfish takeaway, Saint Eleo?" I sneered.

He grinned and pressed his tongue against his cheek. "You got me! What was your grand, saintly revelation you've been withholding, Reverend Alba?" Eleo asked, leaning back in his seat.

"Well, I guess you got me back, I'm curious about those rewards too," I confessed.

"All I can tell you is that any gift from God is far better than any fancy thing that fiancé of yours will ever buy you," he said. I wondered if I heard a hint of jealousy in his voice.

Tongues of Flowers

"You're engaged?" Leah-Jane asked. I nodded. "That's lovely, congratulations. Who is he?" she asked.

"Some Hollywood, hot shot," Eleo interjected.

"I wouldn't say that, exactly. His name's Ted, I moved here with him, he did well in tech and is trying his hand at film now."

Leah-Jane seemed pleased.

The lunch finally ended and Eleo drove me home. Just as he was dropping me off, I surprised myself by saying, "you lied to me."

"What?" he asked.

"You said it 'wasn't like that' with Leah-Jane but it is like that."

"It's complicated."

"You love her." I declared.

"I feel that I should, but I don't know that I do," he blurted out. "You love your fiancé," he added.

"What does that have to do with it?" I asked.

"It has everything to do with it," he said. My stomach dropped.

After a moment of silence, I laughed, downplaying the conversation. "Don't be ridiculous."

CHAPTER TWENTY-ONE

That Night on That Bridge

Late Night Talking by Harry Styles

There was a place on the web, not as deep as one might have expected, where the video could be found. It was all anyone talked about when it happened.

Diamond Yoshida jumping off that bridge.

Ted wasn't home yet. I couldn't sleep. So, for the first time since we'd gotten to Raleigh, I watched it.

Her white dress draped her curvy, goddess-like figure, she pulled her box braids behind her shoulders one last time as she looked down and over the bridge.

And then she jumped.

Apart from the blurry clip, information on the suicide was scarce. I couldn't find any information about there being a letter of any sort.

But she jumped. By herself. She was not pushed.

Tongues of Flowers

Yet my mother's words had made camp in the back of my mind. They think he killed her.

I wondered if Ted drove her mad, and if he would drive me to the same point. I wasn't suicidal. But I had God. And I had Eleo, Nia, Donnie, and Skipper. I wondered, who did she have? The poems suggested a secret lover, why wasn't he enough for her?

I scrolled through Instagram and came across Chad's story. Ted and Yana could be seen in the background again, her arms around him.

The thought of him sleeping next to me and wishing he were with her instead of me was wretched and agonizing in every way. There wasn't a person I'd want to be compared to less than a famous actress.

My phone started ringing. Eleo.

"Hello?" I answered, sitting at the edge of our leather couch.

"Alba, hey! Sorry to bother you, I know it's super late, uh, but how are you?"

It was midnight.

"You're no bother, I'm okay. You?" I asked, walking out to the backyard.

"That's good, yeah, I'm doing well. What are you thinking about?" he asked.

I laughed as I paced back and forth. "Eleo, did you call me just to ask what I'm thinking about? What does it matter to you what an engaged woman is thinking about in the middle of the night?" I asked, somewhat regretting that I brought the engagement up, but it was true.

Tongues of Flowers

"You're right, I'm sorry, I just had this weird feeling. I couldn't stop worrying about you, I thought something was wrong," he said.

"I'm fine, you must have over-spiritualized it," I said, I stopped pacing. "Sounds like you can't stop thinking about me." What is wrong with me? Why would I say that?

He cleared his throat. "I don't know about all that."

"I'm only kidding, Eleo."

"So am I," he said, still in an unusually serious tone.

"Well, I'm fine, so… rest well," I said, hanging up the phone before he could reply.

Ugh, that was so awkward, Lord! Why was I talking like that?

I dipped my feet into the pool.

What am I going to do? Where am I supposed to go? You wouldn't suggest I stay here, would you, Lord?

I looked back and forth from our room on the second floor to the garden gate. It occurred to me I could leave. But then where would I go?

I couldn't bare going back to Hampstead, "I told you so," from my mom and begging for my awful job back and my mom's boyfriend-of-the-week treating us like dirt. And I feared if I went back, I may be stuck for good.

I thought about asking Nia if I could stay with her. But as much as Nia meant to me, she didn't really know me. She likely had no idea how much she meant to me. I couldn't ask that much of her. Alaska seemed to be the best option, but what was there for me? A busy, hard-headed brother who abandoned me to begin with?

Tongues of Flowers

And there was a reason I came to Raleigh with Ted. I loved him that day that he asked me to join him. *I know he's sick, but sicknesses get healed every day.*

CHAPTER TWENTY-TWO

Spirits Consumed After Dark

Duvet by Bôa

Ted finally arrived home. He was drunk again.

You'd think I would've learned by then that Ted should be avoided once the moon was shining and the spirits had been consumed. You'd think.

"I want you to go to therapy," I said.

"Couples therapy? We never fight," he said, pausing by the fridge, throwing me a stern look.

"We do, well you fight me I just don't fight back."

"You gotta be f'ck'n kidding me. Poor you! Sweet Alba who stays home and does nothing all day! Who doesn't have to pay for anything!" Ted said, throwing his arms in the air.

"I have a job, if you want rent, I'm happy to pay it," I said.

Tongues of Flowers

"Oh, great. Great. You don't make in a year what this house costs per month, Alba. I don't need your money and I don't need therapy; I need you to be grateful for once!" He cried, slamming his hand against the counter. "I'm so stressed out and you're so ungrateful!" he whined.

"I'm grateful you got me out of Hampstead, okay? Really, I am, I thank you all the time. But that doesn't dismiss the fact that sometimes you scare me," I said, my voice was stern, but my eyes were on the ground.

"I SCARE you?! Seriously?"

"You hit me the other night, and have thrown stuff and been weird," I said.

"THAT is what you're talking about? Oh my fu–Alba, have you met an actual victim? You are so embarrassing," he said, running his hands into his hair, grasping his skull. "I thought your mom had all these dudes mess with you guys, I'd think you'd know what actual abuse is," he added.

"I hate you, Ted," I said, tears streaming down my face.

"Don't cry, don't f'ck'n cry," he started pacing around the kitchen.

My sobbing grew hysterical. He grabbed my shoulders and pulled me out of the chair, causing us both to fall to the floor. Still clenching my shoulders, he slammed my body onto the ground again, sitting on top of me. "IS THAT WHAT YOU WANT?" he groaned.

I put my hands over my mouth and closed my eyes. He cupped my face with his hands. "Stop crying!" he said again, squeezing my face, painfully.

Tongues of Flowers

"Leave me alone, please," I said, still closing my eyes.

"You want to be a victim so bad, huh?!"

"Ted, please…" I whimpered.

"Okay." He got off me and took a few steps toward the trash can before puking. I scooted into the nearest closet and locked the door.

I sat there in the dark, on the floor, praying so quietly I'm not sure I even spoke aloud.

How will you save me from this?

After about 20 minutes Ted knocked on the closet door. "Alba, come to bed," he moaned.

I didn't say anything. I hoped he would think I was asleep. It worked.

CHAPTER TWENTY-THREE

Nerah Lane

Moon Song by Phoebe Bridgers

The next morning, I walked out of the closet and Ted was sitting at the table, all cleaned up and beautiful. Even the light fell on him just right.

"Come eat," he said, standing up and pulling out a chair next to him. I sat down. "I'm sorry about last night, I was just really tired and stressed from work and I drank too much, I shouldn't have been rude though," he said. He had been more than rude, but I didn't care to argue.

"It's fine," I said, unsure of what I could say.

"I got you this," he said, pulling out a black, Nerah Lane box. He opened it to reveal a gorgeous, regal, diamond strutted necklace. Never in my life did I think I would see a Nerah Lane necklace in the flesh, let alone own one.

"Jeez."

He gently pulled my hair back and put the necklace on me. I flinched as the necklace hit a bruise on the back of my neck. He froze

Tongues of Flowers

and gave me a look that made me feel like I should keep quiet. "Let's see how it looks," he finally said, holding my hand and guiding me to the mirror. He wrapped his arms around me as we stood in front of the mirror. I looked hideous next to him, like a wet rat with a gazelle. Or a pig in pearls.

"Thank you," I said.

CHAPTER TWENTY-FOUR

Lotus on Trapeze

But You Won't Love a Ghost by Emarosa

Donnie invited all of us to her show. Her band had a new name, "Lotus on Trapeze."

I surprised myself by inviting Ted. We were in a weird place. After the kitchen incident, we had a good few days. But it was strange, I concealed the bruises well, and they were fading, but I still knew what he had done.

Part of me hoped he would go on another trip soon, I had trouble sleeping when he was there, and I couldn't think clearly. I needed to plan, to reevaluate my life.

Ted looked so polished compared to everyone else there, but in a cool and natural way. I would have bet every girl there was jealous of me.

He wrapped his arm around my shoulder, and we headed toward the venue. Just as we were walking in I saw Eleo sprawled out

Tongues of Flowers

on the ground outside the building. He was eating a cheeseburger with a homeless man.

"That's Eleo," I said. Ted spared a glance and then continued heading toward the door.

"Should we go say hi?" I asked, my eyes still on Eleo.

"No, he'll find us inside, it's fine, let's see if we can get seats," he said. I complied.

We joined Skipper by the bar. It was strange seeing Ted and Skipper meeting each other, worlds colliding.

The first band to play was much heavier than Lotus on Trapeze. Ted and Skipper talked about Ted's film. Skipper mentioned his tech skills and that he'd love to take a look at their equipment, Ted nearly offered him a job. Quite a different response from when I mentioned being the writer's room errand girl.

"Who's going to join me in the pit?" I asked.

"I'm waiting for my drink," Skipper said, pointing to the bartender.

Ted shook his head. I frowned.

"Okay," Ted laughed. "I got you," he said, extending his hand to help me off my stool. He held my hand as we maneuvered through the crowd, it appeared their demographic was exclusively men descended from Goliath, so I was glad for his guidance.

Oh, great, I'm even thinking in biblical references now, what have you done to me, Lord?

As Ted pulled me through the crowd, I watched the back of his head and felt guilty. I felt guilty that I still liked having him in my line of vision, and I liked the security of knowing, even if only as a

Tongues of Flowers

technicality, that I was his. Yet whenever he touched me my stomach twisted, and I wanted to pull away. But oftentimes when you pull things apart, they break even more.

Ted wrapped his arm around me while we listened, I held on tight to his shirt. I closed my eyes and tried to pretend I was just a girl at a show with a boy she loved, nothing more and nothing less. The fictionality of it all didn't stop my heart from pounding, my breath from shallowing, or my palms from perspiring.

Ted gestured to his phone and then walked away. "I got to take this," he mouthed.

I tried to follow him out but got lost in the crowd.

I bumped into a middle-aged man with spiky hair. He looked back and forth from me to the mosh pit and then smiled, wide and toothless.

I followed his stare and shook my head profusely. He giggled and pushed me into the mosh pit.

The first person to crash into me was a short girl with a pixie haircut and lots of chains. I shouldered her back and headed for the crowd, but not before a 6'5 linebacker-type flung himself at the person next to me, knocking over myself and multiple other people on the outskirts of the pit.

I was on the floor, looking up at passing black shadows with a backdrop of red and orange lights. Suddenly Eleo was next to me crouched down. "Do you want me to carry you?" he asked. It didn't register to me what he had said until later, so I just looked at him blankly.

He slid one arm under my kneecaps and the other under my back and carried me out of the crowd. He was sweaty, which made

Tongues of Flowers

me think of the day at the beach when we swam beneath the pier. He looked at me, and I felt as if I had been caught in my thoughts.

"I'm fine, I'm fine," I said, squirming in his arms, he set me down.

"Are you sure?"

"Yes."

"Did anyone step on you?"

"No."

"What happened?"

"I accidentally ended up in the mosh pit and Goliath over there felt it was necessary to throw his entire body, horizontal, in my general vicinity," I said, pointing toward the large man in the red onesie.

We stood silent for a moment, and then Eleo started laughing hysterically. I rolled my eyes and tried to contain my smile but ended up in hysterics as well.

We sat on a bench near the side of the stage as they prepared for Donnie's set. Eleo got us drinks. Soda for him, whiskey for me, per my request.

"What were you doing outside with that homeless guy? I asked.

"We were just having some dinner and talking, he's a friend. He lives at the shelter on Peace Street," he said.

"You have homeless friends?" I asked.

"Oh, I have all sorts of friends," he said, winking at me.

"What kind of flower did you give him?" I asked.

"What?" he tilted his head and flashed me a crooked smile.

Tongues of Flowers

"Don't you communicate to all your friends via flowers?" I teased.

His face softened but he maintained a sly grin. He looked down at his lap. "I don't," he admitted softly.

We both turned our attention to the stage as the lights dimmed and Lotus on Trapeze entered the stage. We cheered her on as loud as we could, applauding our hands red, giving our most to every single song. I taught Eleo the art of crowd surfing. "You just find a group of dudes and gesture up with your thumbs and everyone will throw you around. It's great," I explained.

Eleo's shirt slid up as he rode the crowd, revealing his golden hips, and I found myself blushing and turning away. No, I don't look at people like that anymore, Lord. When I looked up again, I could only see his laugh, because it was bright and everything good in the world was bundled up in it.

We retired to the bench, eventually.

Donnie had a smooth voice, and each song was experimental.

Curious rhymes

On the letter

You slid under my door

I'll keep your secret

Oh you, I couldn't

I couldn't ever quit

Our eyes happened to meet, perhaps the lyrics resonated with each of us too well. I looked away but I could feel him still looking at me.

"Why are you staring at me?" I snapped.

Tongues of Flowers

"Are you going to stay with him?" he asked, sternly. Ignoring my attitude.

"What?"

"Ted. Are you going to stay with him?" Eleo asked again.

"Why wouldn't I?" I replied.

He stared at me for a long moment, his tongue pressing against his cheek. "Never mind," he finally said.

"No, tell me," I said.

"Correct me if I'm wrong but you never bring him to hang out with us, you never talk about him, it just… I don't know. You guys are off," he said.

"It's complicated," I explained.

"Do you guys just see things differently now?" he asked.

"That's part of it, and other things," I said.

"He hasn't hurt you in any way, has he?" Eleo asked, straightening up.

"No! No, of course not," I lied. "What's wrong with you?"

"Oh, okay, sorry," he said, taking a deep breath.

"I think he's cheating on me with an actress he's filming with, I don't know if you've heard of Yana," I said. He hadn't, but he recognized her once I showed him a picture.

"What's stopping you from leaving him?" Eleo asked.

"Well I don't know for sure if he's cheating, there's a lot I don't know about him, I just want the truth," I said.

"I think your gut feeling is adequate proof," he insisted.

Tongues of Flowers

"Well, I don't," I said. He continued explaining why that should be enough, I ignored him and checked my phone. Ted texted me, he was waiting in the car and rushing to head back.

"I have to go, my ride is waiting outside," I said.

"I could take you back," Eleo suggested, following me toward the exit.

"I don't think that would be appropriate in this situation," I replied.

We found Donnie along the way, and I praised her work before heading toward the door.

"Wait!" Eleo called out.

"What?" I paused.

"If you ever need anything, a friend, a getaway car, an accomplice, or whatever, I'm here, I want to help you figure it out," he said.

"Thanks."

CHAPTER TWENTY-FIVE

Blue Lights in My Cage

It's Safe to Say You Dig the Backseat by Dance Gavin Dance

"Sorry, Chad needs me to scan some documents in the home office before midnight," Ted said as we pulled out of the venue.

"No worries, Donnie had just finished."

As we passed the white chapel Ted asked, "is that the seminary your friend Eleo goes to?"

"Yeah, it's pretty, right?" I asked.

"Yeah, it's a shame they waste such a beautiful building on a bunch of sheep," he said.

"Sheep?"

"Ignorant people," Ted clarified.

"I got to the church that meets there," I said.

"Well, that's fine, you're not claiming to be a scholar, but seminary is different, bigotry and ignorance under the guise of academia," he said.

Tongues of Flowers

"Eleo is not ignorant or bigoted, he's kind and intelligent," I said, my blood boiling.

"Trust me, he'd look foolish in a room of philosophers," Ted said.

"Name one philosopher, Ted."

Ted stopped the car in the middle of the highway.

"Ted, what are you doing?" I asked. He remained frozen.

"F'ck you," Ted mouthed, looking at me with half-closed eyes, and I swear I saw specs of red in them.

"Ted, drive! There's cars com–"

We crashed.

No one was hurt, thankfully.

But I still vividly remember the feeling in my chest as the lights got brighter and then the thrust forward.

The police came.

"What happened?" the officer asked.

"I saw a deer in the middle of the road, I couldn't swerve because of another car so I stopped sort of abruptly, sorry about that," Ted lied like it was the most natural thing in the world for him.

Now or never.

"He stopped in the middle of the road because he's insane. He was mad at me so he risked our lives. He's abu–he's crazy," I blurted out. "Help me," I added, looking at the cop with utmost fear.

Ted murmured something to the cop about handling me, and slid him something I couldn't see, the cop said, "All right, you get her home Ted, be careful."

CHAPTER TWENTY-SIX

A Pearl Under Pigs

Me and My Husband by Mitski

Either the cop didn't believe me or didn't care. Ted was so sure that nobody else would either. As soon as we got home, he gave me a wound on my side to ensure I wouldn't forget that.

CHAPTER TWENTY-SEVEN

Poets Don't Cry

Carry Me, Ohio by Sun Kil Moon

"Ocean"

He left me naked at sea

Shut the palace door

And he threw away my key

"Pretty, isn't it," Amanda, one of the ladies who joined my poetry club, said.

"This is by Jae Miko?" I asked. Amanda nodded as she adjusted her ivy cap. "Her works are usually longer, aren't they?"

"Yes, they are! That's why I wanted to bring this one up, it's short so I think it gets lost in her body of work at times. I wanted to know what you guys think of it," Amanda said.

"I like the imagery of the palace and the sea, it creates a very mystical setting," Dante, another new poetry club member, pointed out.

Tongues of Flowers

"Yeah, I agree, it reminds me of the old siren tales," Eleo said.

"I think vulnerability is a big theme, not only in her nakedness, but in the fact that he threw away *her* key," I pondered.

"Yeah, I didn't notice the key part being *her* key. That must have been very intentional, she could have put *the* key. It fits with the nakedness," Amanda mused.

"Exactly! That's why I was thinking this is about her ex-husband, Bernard Apheet, they lived on the west coast for a time, I believe. I could totally see this narrative being that she met him with old wounds, and she trusted Bernard despite that, and he encouraged her to feel safe and heal her wounds, only to rip them back open and use her own vulnerabilities against her," I ranted.

Eleo leaned back in his seat with his pen at the corner of his mouth, watching me closely.

I had this deep sense, that it was time to allow a level of luminosity to reach the shadow that I had been coexisting with. If I were ever to begin to dispel it, the time was now.

After the meeting had ended, I walked up to Eleo and placed the plant I had been carrying around for days in in his hands.

"Wolfsbane," he whispered to himself.

Wolfsbane- A foe is near

CHAPTER TWENTY-EIGHT

Specs of Green

Ivy by Taylor Swift (non-explicit version)

Eleo took my hand and quietly led me into the woods behind the bookstore until we were deep enough that we could not be heard. He placed the Wolfsbane on the ground between us.

"What aren't you telling me?" he asked.

"Ted was married to someone before me. His wife's name was Diamond Wilson. She committed suicide, threw herself off a bridge," I began to explain. "Allegedly."

"You don't think it was a suicide?"

"I mean, it was caught on video, it was dark and grainy, but she did jump. The thing is, around that time he cut off ties with his family and just started acting differently... so people started to speculate he had gone crazy, and drove Diamond to suicide, somehow. But I dismissed it as him mourning his wife and wanting a fresh start but then I found some poems that Diamond wrote... she was having an affair, and Ted can... have a temper, and living with him now, I wouldn't rule out him having some serious mental health issues," I said.

"Has he hurt you, Alba? Don't lie to me, please," Eleo said.

"No, Eleo, stop asking me that. I'm fine, really." It was a lie, which made me want to kick myself, but I couldn't bring myself to say it.

Eleo took a step closer to me and gently cupped my face with his potent hands. "Please, leave him. You have me, and Nia, and the church… we will help you," he said. I shook my head. He dropped to his knees and held my hands, looking up at me earnestly. I had never heard him sound so serious. "Alba, I am begging you. I am on my knees, begging you. Please do not go back to him," he said, in a deeper and more desperate voice than I had known him capable of.

I pulled my hands away and turned the opposite way. "I can't," I said, my voice cracking.

He stood up and went to face me again. "What is stopping you?!" he probed.

"Many things, but for one, I need to know the truth, unless I have irrefutable proof that something happened, which it may not have, it could happen again to someone else," I said.

"That's not your burden," he replied. "Alba, I don't know what I can say to keep you from him–" I backed him into a tree, putting my hands over his mouth to shut him up.

"Eleo! Stop it. I didn't tell you because I'm leaving him," I said, removing my hands from his mouth.

"Why did you tell me, then?" he asked.

"I was hoping, maybe you could help me figure out the truth about Ted," I said.

Tongues of Flowers

"On one condition," he said.

"Okay…"

"If he ever touches you or says anything threatening, you leave him and come stay with me or Nia."

I agreed. Amidst the green moss and the sound of chirping birds, we shook hands. Having Eleo on my side, even if he didn't know the full story, gave me a sense of relief.

Lord, is he an angel?

CHAPTER TWENTY-NINE

Made for This

Your Love is Like by Rick Pino

I sang to God.

That evening I locked myself in Ted's library and I sang, not in a particularly nice sounding manner, but with utmost sincerity. This had become a regular occurrence for me, and it was surely the saving grace that pulled me through those despondent nights.

I would sing the same line of some worship song over and over. A request or complaint seldom failed to make an appearance but were quickly overshadowed with enchantment, expressing itself in adoration.

It was a room of treasures, not because of anything in it, but because it was just Him and I.

And even with all my short-sightedness and distractedness, I was beginning to realize that any room I was in, at any moment, no matter what I was doing, could be that room.

CHAPTER THIRTY

The Ever-Unfolding Plan

Play Date by Melanie Martinez (Clean Version)

Ted's office was the natural first place to look, unfortunately, he kept a security camera in front of it to ensure nobody went in, including me.

But in true divine fashion, God provided us with Skipper, who managed to gain access to the security cameras. To not alarm Ted, we would only allow ourselves five minutes to keep the cameras shut off.

Donnie would park her car at the start of the neighborhood so she could warn us if Ted pulled into the driveway. His schedule was sporadic, so there was no truly convenient time to do it. He came and went as he pleased and did not take kindly to requests for a schedule. That was also the only day of the week there was no hired help in the house.

"Okay, the cameras are off, you guys should be good," Skipper said through the walkie.

Tongues of Flowers

Eleo and I quickly climbed out of Donnie's car. "Be careful, and fast," Donnie said before driving to the entrance of the neighborhood.

Eleo and I entered the house. "Seems like a lot for two people," he said.

I led us to the office and Eleo was able to pick the lock in a nerve-racking minute. The office was cluttered with various film figurines, empty bottles of alcohol, and miscellaneous documents.

We weren't sure exactly what we were looking for. An incriminating picture or credit card bill or journal, maybe?

We quickly slammed through the dark, wooden drawers and cabinets. One of the drawers at first glance seemed to only have a few irrelevant documents, but I opened it wider than one normally would and noticed an opening in the back revealing a secret compartment.

I removed the top wooden piece that concealed the compartment and saw a couple photographs on the bottom. I immediately recognized Diamond's face in one, she was in a gray sweatshirt, smiling and tilting her head. I also saw a photograph of a dark-haired man from behind. There was also a drawing, I couldn't make it out, but it was drawn with crayon.

"I think I might have something," I said.

Eleo peaked his head over. "Yeah, what are those?"

I went to grab the pile of photos, but as I pulled the drawer fully out to reach in, the whole thing blew up into flames, which sent me stumbling backward.

I didn't realize I was still screaming until Eleo grabbed my arms. "We need to get out of here," he said, pulling me up.

Tongues of Flowers

"One minute, guys," Skipper said through the walkie.

We passed a window on the way to the door, and I saw a black convertible pulling in. "Shi–how is he here?" I panicked.

It turned out Ted had taken the backroads that day, so Donnie never saw him enter.

We sprinted out of the house and through backyard, heading straight for the woods. Eleo held my hand firmly as we ran.

"You guys set the office on fire?!" Skipper blurted through the walkie. Neither of us replied.

On the other side of the woods, Donnie's car was waiting for us just as we had planned if Ted came home.

"What the hell happened in there?" Donnie asked as she merged back onto the road.

I stared out the window, bewildered and breathless.

"I–I don't–I don't know," Eleo stuttered.

We were silent until we arrived at the bookstore. We unlocked the doors and headed toward the break room and sat around the rectangular, wooden table.

"There was a hidden compartment in one of the drawers, and there were some photographs of people on the bottom, I took out the drawer so I could reach the photos but it…exploded," I said.

"What?" Donnie gasped, throwing her hand over her heart.

"This needs to be proof enough, Alba," Eleo said.

"It doesn't prove anything, I'm just more confused," I said.

"If he sets up a… I don't know, basically a bomb, to protect a secret drawer of photographs, he is not sane."

Tongues of Flowers

"We don't know that he set it up, it could've been a weird...I don't know..."

My phone started ringing. It was Ted.

Me: Hello?

Ted: Where are you?

Me: I'm at the bookstore. You?

Ted: I knew it. I knew it.

Me: What?

Ted: The bookstore is closed on Sundays.

Me: Nia wanted me to do some inventory stuff.

Ted: Don't lie to me.

Me: I'm not.

Ted: Who is with you? What were you looking for in my office?

Me: I don't know what you're talking about, I never went in your office, I've been working.

Ted: Well, SOMEONE screwed with the cameras and went f'ck'ng around in my office and now the house is on fire!

Me: W-what? Are you...okay?

Ted: No.

And then he hung up the phone.

Eleo shook his head and stormed out of the breakroom. I followed him out, he was dialing 911 on his phone. I put my hand over his. "Don't," I said.

"I have to," he whispered.

Tongues of Flowers

"I need more time, Eleo. I need undeniable proof that something is wrong," I said.

"Let's just try talking to the police, maybe they have suspicions and ca–"

"No, Eleo."

He gave me a puzzled look. "Why not?" he asked.

"I already tried talking to the police, they didn't care," I explained.

"But now we can tell them about the photographs," he said.

"Eleo, no. Stop it. This is my life and my relationship, and you do not get to make these decisions," I asserted, I headed towards the breakroom and grabbed my bag. "Donnie, can you take me back?" I asked.

"Are you sure?" she asked with a frown.

"Yes, it's fine, he hasn't done anything to me, and I can hold my own weight. Please," I said. She agreed. Eleo left the building without a word.

CHAPTER THIRTY-ONE

People Either Will Love or Hate This Part

On the Way Down by Ryan Cabrera

By the time I arrived the fire department was pulling out. Ted was sitting on the porch with a flask.

"Are you okay?" I asked.

He looked at me with puffy eyes and stretched out his arm, motioning for me to sit next to him. I obeyed.

"It only got the office, the rest of the house is okay," he said.

"That's good."

"Someone shut down our cameras and went into my office," he continued.

"And then they set it on fire?" I asked.

He pursed his lips. "If the fire department or anyone were to ask, yes," he said. "But no," he added.

Tongues of Flowers

"I don't understand, what happened then?"

He removed his arm from around me and leaned back on his wrists. "I'm telling you this because I trust you, okay?"

"Okay."

"I set up a trigger in one of the drawers to protect my scripts from being stolen," he said.

"Does that mean the scripts are gone now?" I asked.

"I'd rather them be no one's than be someone else's. But anyway, it was probably a robbery, go check if any of your stuff is missing, we'll have to let the police know tomorrow if we can't find anything," he said.

I went up to my bathroom and slid my Nerah Lane necklace into my pocket without even thinking about it, I needed Ted to believe it was a robbery. I continued to pretend to search the house. When I finished, Ted was setting out dinner plates. "Hungry?"

"Not really," I said.

"Was everything where you left it?" he asked.

"I can't find my Nerah Lane necklace, I think they took it."

Ted dropped the plate he was holding. "You're a liar," he said, with a cynical grin.

"What?"

"I looked through your jewelry, I just saw the Nerah Lane. You're a liar," he said, chuckling.

Lord, I'm afraid. Help me.

"Maybe I missed it, I'm just flustered from everything," I said, turning around to go pretend to look again.

Tongues of Flowers

The laughing stopped. He ran up behind me and slammed me to the ground. I closed my eyes and screeched so loud, I hadn't even heard the other presence enter the room.

Suddenly, Ted was flung off me.

I sat up to find Eleo on top of Ted, he gave him two punches, knocking him out cold. He went for another punch but I ran over and grabbed Eleo's wrist.

"Eleo!" I cried.

"Are you okay?" he asked, his eyes were huge and his breaths deep I didn't know what to say. "Let's go, Alba," he said. He took my hand and led me out the door.

CHAPTER THIRTY-TWO

Stay with Me

I'll Never Let You Go by Zach Webb

We arrived at Nia's house, and I had nothing but the knitted sweatshirt, denim skirt, and combat boots I was wearing, my wallet, and the Nerah Lane necklace in my pocket.

Nia set a bowl of soup in front of me as I told her everything… including all the other times Ted hurt me. Eleo was leaning against the kitchen counter listening, his head lowered as I told the truth.

"The safest place would probably be a woman's shelter for victims of domestic violence," Nia said.

"No, I can't. I went to one when I was a little girl, I went with my mom because of one of her ex-boyfriends… we were even worse off there." I shuddered at the memory, the cold floor, the kicking…

"I know a lady at the one here, Alba, this one is very secure, they would take good care of you," she insisted. I refused.

"Well, you're welcome to stay here," Nia said. "I just really think that's the safest bet. But we can figure that out later, you just stay here tonight and get some rest, my room is right over there, okay? And you're here in the guest room," she said pointing to another room. I thanked her.

"I'll sleep on the couch if that's okay," I heard Eleo say to Nia as I ate my soup.

"Yeah, you don't want to go home?" she asked.

"I don't want to leave her," he said.

I couldn't sleep. It felt good to be out of Ted's house. I liked Nia's clean sheets. I liked the sound of Eleo tossing and turning in the living room. I wasn't so naive to think that my troubles were over, everything was in the air. More than my thoughts could even begin to sort through. Nevertheless.

I haven't done much, even since meeting You. I haven't devoted hours of my life to the homeless or even gotten my GED… all I have really wanted since I saw You is to know You more. And I'm sure You're in all those things in some complex way, and if You decide to get me out of this somehow, I think I would like to find You in those things, and in anything that You would show me. Whenever, whatever, just make sure You're there.

Thank you.

I woke up startled in the middle of the night. I had a nightmare that I was shaking on the floor and everything was pitch black, and a voice was yelling at me to get back in bed, I said I was scared. The voice replied, "so what? You're gonna go tell everyone I'm abusive now?!" I was afraid of the voice. It grabbed me. I hadn't realized it, but I must have screamed as I woke up because Eleo ran in.

"Alba, what's wrong?" he asked, sweetly.

Tongues of Flowers

"Nothing," I said, but for some reason, I started crying. And I couldn't stop.

He sat on the edge of the bed.

"I'm sorry," I choked out.

"No, no... you have nothing to be sorry for," he said. My crying grew harsher, and I laid back down, plummeting into the pillow to hide my face. He held my hand gently.

"Will you come here, come be here with me?" I asked.

"Okay." He adjusted himself onto the bed and wrapped both of his arms around me from behind. "It's okay, you're safe now, I promise," he whispered.

"I was so scared of him for so long, Somehow, I didn't even realize it until now," I said, through choppy breaths. One of his arms was around my waist, the other arm went across my collarbones to my shoulder. He rubbed my arm gently and I could feel his face near the back of my head.

"Alba, I'm so sorry," he said. "Does me holding you help, or do you want me to let go or leave or go get you anything?" he asked.

"Stay with me," I said. "Will you stay with me like this?" I asked.

"Okay," he said. I ran my fingers over his forearms and took a deep breath. My breathing was finally beginning to regulate.

That was the first time, maybe ever, that I truly felt safe.

CHAPTER THIRTY-THREE

The Rigged, the Rabid, and the Running

Out Loud by Scarypoolparty

That morning I made my cup of tea and sat by Nia's back porch.

I will exalt you, Lord,
for you lifted me out of the depths
and did not let my enemies gloat over me.
Lord my God, I called to you for help,
and you healed me.
You, Lord, brought me up from the realm of the dead;
you spared me from going down to the pit.
Psalm 30

"What are you reading?" Nia asked.

"Psalm 30," I said, closing the leather Bible Eleo had gifted me.

"What do you think?" she asked as she sat next to me.

Tongues of Flowers

"I feel as if I could have written it. I cannot believe he got me out of there, I felt like I was paralyzed, I thought I would die living like that," I said.

Though I still refused the shelter, we did go file a police report. Nia didn't give me much of an option. The officers didn't say much, except that they would follow up with us.

On the way back I had Nia stop at the pawn shop and I sold them my Nerah Lane necklace, I walked out with a check for $10k. That was more than I expected, which was good because I knew a fresh start was at hand.

When we got to the house Donnie was standing on Nia's porch.

"Why haven't any of you answered your phones?" she asked.

"Oh, shoot, sorry," Eleo said, looking at the missed calls on his screen.

"Look at this," she said, handing me her phone.

It was a video of Ted on his Instagram, posted that morning. He gave this outlandish story about how I was "having an affair" with Eleo and we "set the house on fire" and "attacked him." His black eye added a level of pathos to the story. The video had 2 million views already. And the comments were avidly on his side.

None of us said anything for a long while. "But, you guys filed the police report before he posted, so that should be helpful for your case," Donnie eventually said.

"Yeah."

Skipper called to inform Nia that the bookstore had been vandalized with slurs targeted toward me. I began to feel very guilty, though Nia assured me I didn't need to.

Tongues of Flowers

Then Eleo got a call from his seminary. They told him he could not come to class, indefinitely, considering the allegations. Then I began to feel even guiltier.

Finally, an officer came to our door, I hoped maybe he would tell us they were handling Ted. But rather, the officer told us Ted was granted an emergency restraining order against Eleo and I, and he sternly warned us to stay away from Ted.

I erupted in tears and ran out of the room. I heard Eleo say to the officer, "Why are you treating her like the bad guy? She is a victim!"

Donnie followed me into the room. "I'm so sorry, Alba," she said, stroking my hair out of my face. "What are you going to do?" she asked.

And I knew.

Just promise wherever I end up You'll be there too, okay, Lord?

CHAPTER THIRTY-FOUR

Wherever He Might Lead

It's a Wonderful Life by John Lucas

The first person I told my plan to was Donnie, and I swore her to secrecy. "You'll need to disguise yourself," she said. Before we knew it she had scissors in one hand and black dye in the other.

Eleo passed by the doorway as I ran my fingers through my new shoulder-length black hair. We made eye contact, and he gave me a puzzled look. "Just felt like a change," I said.

"It looks nice," he said, his eyes tired.

The next person I told was Skipper, he helped me secure fake documents. The Nerah Lane money went through and I was able to secure a social security card, driver's license, and passport. I wasn't planning to go international, but it was nice to have the option.

Then I told Nia. "Where will you go? With your brother in Alaska?" she asked.

"No, he'd guess that. Somewhere random," I said.

"Did you tell Eleo yet?"

Tongues of Flowers

"Not yet," I admitted. She sighed.

That evening, just as I was thinking about how to tell Eleo, he came into the guest room and sat next to me.

"Eleo, I'm leaving. I got some documents and money and I am leaving soon, maybe this weekend," I admitted.

"You're leaving tomorrow," he said quietly.

"What?"

He handed me a plane ticket to Mexico City. "Tomorrow morning I'm going to take you to the airport. You're going to land in Mexico City and my cousin Maria and her husband Julio are going to meet you there. They live deep in the mountains on our family land, Cabeza del Toro. You'll be safe there and can start over," he said.

"How did you…"

"Our friends are not very good at keeping secrets," he said.

"Thank you, Eleo. I'm so sorry I dragged you into all this," I said.

"No, I'm sorry I didn't see what was happening, I'm sorry I didn't do something sooner," he lamented.

CHAPTER THIRTY-FIVE

Until Planets Align

Gold Rush by Taylor Swift

Eleo went over the details extensively in the car, and then we walked into the bustling airport silently. He walked me as far as he could go.

"It's best if we don't contact each other," he said.

"Ever?"

"I don't know," he said, putting his hands over his eyes and turning away. I wrapped my arms around him and rested my head on his chest.

"Can't you come with me?" I asked.

"I'm not leaving until he's in prison or worse," Ted explained.

"I want to help you," I said, which wasn't entirely true. I did want to be with Eleo. I wanted Ted to be in jail. But I could feel that most deeply, at that moment, I needed something else.

Tongues of Flowers

"You are helping, you going away will eventually cause Ted to bring his guard down and then I can get a better look," he explained.

I shut my eyes to hold back tears. "Aw," he said, as he put my head to his chest again. "You're going to have so much fun there, it'll be a fresh start for you, it'll be so good and you will be so happy and safe," he said. I nodded and pulled away.

He handed me an envelope. "Just a farewell letter," he said.

"Okay," I said. I took my bag from him. "I should start heading through security now," I said.

"Okay," he said. We stood silently facing one another. He leaned down and kissed my cheek, I must have been the bloodiest shade of red. "I… am going to be praying for you," he added. I thanked him and turned around.

We both started walking away and then it dawned on me that I would never see Eleo Hernandez again.

"Eleo," I said, turning around. He was already looking back at me.

He walked up to me. My heart was beating as fast as his hands were slipping around my neck. He inhaled a slow and steady breath, looking at my lips, and he exhaled, looking into my eyes, which were begging for him.

I knew the moment his soft, rose-blush lips touched mine that he had to be an angel, just as I had suspected, and no evil could have pried my body from his. The thumb of his brawny hand tenderly stroked my cheek as our lips parted, and I was reminded that he is just a man, and I am just a woman, and neither of us had yet truly met heaven. He was just a glorious taste.

"I love you," he said, barely above a whisper.

Tongues of Flowers

"You love me?" I asked.

"Helplessly, foolishly, and unfortunately in nearly every regard," he confessed.

"I love you."

Before either of us knew it, Eleo was fifteen minutes down the road from the airport, strategizing in his apartment and I was flying south of the border, to my new home.

As I was sitting on the airplane, I opened the envelope to find a letter and pieces of little white flowers which I identified as white kalanchoes.

White Kalanchoe- persistence and eternal love

CHAPTER THIRTY-SIX

Blessings, Eleo

Egypt by Cory Asbury

Alba,

I am sorry that nothing has gone as it ought to have for you. If you were to ask me why you have been given the lot that you have, I would not have a good answer for you, maybe one day I will, but right now I don't.

And I don't know what I would have done if you hadn't agreed to leave, because I won't have peace until you're gone. And if I walk into the bookstore tomorrow, and I stand in the spot where I used to watch you trace your fingers along the edges of the shelves, and I find that I won't know peace until you're back, I still will say nothing.

I want to kill him. I know that is not virtuous on my end, and I'm ashamed to say that's not even what's keeping me from doing it. What's keeping me from doing it is you. If I were to kill Ted, it would only solidify his absurd narrative of us conspiring against him, and

Tongues of Flowers

you would likely lose your freedom right alongside me. I sound like a madman! I never used to think like this, you know.

What I wanted to tell you is that you will be safe in Cabeza del Toro. I promise. Please don't be afraid. I hope you grow incredibly close to God while you're there. I saw you were reading Joshua on your break the other day. Well, I have this suspicion that God Himself is the real promised land. And you have Him now. You get to take Him with you. And if you come back? Still, there He will be.

I would also like you to know that I love you… and me buying you a ticket away and insisting we not speak is out of an overflow of love for you. If I loved you a rational amount, I would just want you with me, but a reckless amount? Well, that'll push you off the edge, knowing there's nowhere safer you could land than in the will of God.

Blessings,

Eleo

PS. Read Psalm 23

CHAPTER THIRTY-SEVEN

Cabeza del Toro

Lobo-Hombre en Paris by La Union

I spent a total of 3 years in Cabeza del Toro.

There were many points when I thought I would stay there forever.

Julio and Maria treated me well. Maria, who was only 7 years older than I, took particular interest in discipling me. It seemed there was a lesson in everything, from feeding the chickens to hanging the laundry to dry.

Spiritually, I had fallen deeply in love with God, irrevocably so. We attended the small, local house church three times a week, which was beautiful. We sang, shared stories, met each other's needs, and served the little community together. Seeing the guys with their guitars out often made me miss Eleo.

But my most blissful spiritual moments were not even those, I spent much of my time adventuring in the mountains with God. We'd talk, or sing, or draw, sometimes I brought a book. I loved

Tongues of Flowers

Him. I swear one of those days in the fields, looking up at the vast skies, something in me healed.

And then there was Mateo.

I could hear his motorcycle from a mile away, there was no real road on our mountain, so it hit rock after rock along the dirt path.

"Princesa," he yelled as he stopped the bike next to me. "Hi," he added, as he ran his fingers through his dark hair.

"Hola Mateo," I said as I closed the gate to the chicken coop.

"I'm heading into town, c'mon."

When we arrived in town we stopped in a downtown building where he went to pay his property tax. In Cabeza del Toro it was nearly impossible to get phone signal or internet connection, I hadn't even bothered with a phone since I'd been there.

Afterward, we headed to a restaurant.

"I was wondering when I would see your beautiful face again, Hermosa!" Ernesto, the elderly owner, said. He pinched my face to his amusement.

"Ay, don't tell me you're with this loser," one of the men said, pointing his corona at Mateo, who whacked him in the back of the head.

"Don't listen to him," Mateo said with a wink.

"We're not together anyway," I said.

"OHH!" Ernesto and the man with the corona both busted into a fit of laughter.

"Yeah, yeah, I'm working on it, okay?" Mateo said, rolling his eyes.

Tongues of Flowers

"Okay, Okay," Ernesto said, still giggling.

As we were eating, I happened to glance up at the TV. A reporter said, "...controversial director Jonabee Isaac, husband of esteemed actress Yana, has been found decapitated. No suspects have been identified at this time..."

I flung my hand over my mouth.

"What? What's wrong?" Mateo asked.

"I have to go home," I said.

"Okay... let me just go pay Ernesto..."

"No, Mateo, I mean I have to go back to the US."

CHAPTER THIRTY-EIGHT

Out Yonder, Where the Mermaids Cry

Carolina in my Mind by John Denver

I didn't tell Eleo or anyone else from the bookstore that I was returning. I didn't know what their lives looked like after three years. I didn't want to intrude. I ensured that Julio and Maria also didn't tell anyone.

During those three years, during the holidays I would sometimes go to an internet cafe and send my brother a vague email, so he knew I was alive. He was displeased with my distance and lack of details.

But I knew he had moved back to North Carolina and gotten a house there and my mother lived with him. He retired from the military and was working as a mechanic in Hampstead.

I walked through the doors of their two-story blue house, it was simple, but much nicer than anything we ever lived in growing up.

Tongues of Flowers

"Alba!" Loo yelled from the garage as he ran towards me. He pulled me in for a hug, it felt strange, I couldn't remember ever hugging my brother except for when he left for the military many, many years ago.

My mother was in the kitchen, baking, I couldn't believe it. She looked much healthier than I had ever seen her. "Don't ever disappear like that again," she said.

"I told you and Loo that I was okay, mama, and I really was, better than ever, but I'm sorry. I didn't mean to worry you. But you look well," I said.

"You seem so different," she said, looking me up and down. "You've changed," she added, astonished.

I laughed. "We're supposed to, mama."

That night was the best night I had ever had with my family. We played card games and ate dinner together. A simple pleasure, but something I hadn't known could be.

Lord, you can restore anything, can't you?

The next morning, before I could even begin to conceive a plan of action, my mother yelled from downstairs, "Alba, someone's at the door for you!"

"Just a second!" I threw on a sundress and took the towel off my head before running downstairs.

Standing in the doorway was a familiar face, and my chest filled up.

"Eleo."

CHAPTER THIRTY-NINE

The Dynamic Duo Returns

Tis The Damn Season by Taylor Swift

Eleo walked through the front door, tall and in uniform.

"You're a cop now," I said.

"Evidently so."

We headed to the back porch, a sunlit room filled with greenery and tall windows. I poured us each a glass of lemonade.

"Mint and cucumber? That's how my mother used to make it," he said.

"It's your grandmother's recipe, originally," I said, taking a sip myself.

He looked down and laughed, shaking his head. His hair was short and clean-cut. His jaw was sharper and his shoulders broader. "It's strange we haven't spoken in years, but you know my family better than I do now."

"Eleo, how did you know I was back?" I asked.

Tongues of Flowers

"Maria told Julio who told Juanita who told her milkman who told Lila who told my abuela who told me, I think, maybe not quite in that order." He grinned.

"And how did you find our address, and why are you here?" I asked.

"I could track you down anywhere, Alba. I'm here for the same reason that you're back," he said.

"You heard about Yana's husband?"

He nodded. "So, you want to reopen this mystery? See if we can expose Ted?" I asked.

"I never closed that mystery; I've been trying to expose him since you left." He sighed.

"Eleo, what exactly happened after I left? Start from the beginning."

CHAPTER FORTY

Tongues of Towns

Dancing with Our Hands Tied by Taylor Swift

Donnie moved to LA to pursue music. Skipper got a fancy tech job, he was still around, but he upgraded from his mom's basement to a fancy condo downtown. Nia was still running the bookstore, which was doing well enough. They all kept in touch, but it wasn't as it was.

Ted got wrapped up in the hustle of fame and moved to LA, so the allegations toward Eleo never came to fruition, but still, Eleo's seminary never welcomed him back. He ended up in the police academy, with a resolve to eventually become a detective.

He never stopped investigating Ted.

Eleo hit a dead end while trying to uncover more about Diamond. He did manage to find three poems she published online under a pseudonym, "D.L.L." The poems were published just a couple of days before her death. Though their meanings weren't clear at the time, it was clear that there was more to the story.

Tongues of Flowers

While Eleo was investigating Diamond, he realized there was another mysterious death in Ted's life, the death of his brother, Lee Yoshida. Information about Lee was so scarce online, it was like he never existed. There was simply an obituary by the family, stating that Lee died of an overdose at 18 years old, 5 years before Diamond's death.

Eleo visited Hampstead several times to question people about the death of Lee, but Hampstead didn't take well to strangers, especially not ones digging up town dirt. And of course, the Yoshida's wealth bought them ownership of the tongues of the town.

"And now I'm here," he finally said.

"Hampstead doesn't take well to strangers, but I'm not a stranger."

"You think you could get some more information out of the locals?" he asked.

"I could try, I wasn't exactly popular, but I think I know a couple of people I could ask," I said.

"As a team?" he asked, extending his hand.

"A team," I agreed, placing my hand in his, realizing how much I had missed his touch.

I wanted more, but the passage of time brought about this strange unknowingness. I wouldn't dare ask if he now belonged to another, I didn't want to hear it. Especially not if it was Leah-Jane. I had learned to be okay without him, I could do it again, if need be. But I would rather him be a friend in my life than nothing at all.

CHAPTER FORTY-ONE

Artisan of Dreams and the Girl Hanging from His String

Illicit Affairs by Taylor Swift

"A Wasted Life"

Our failing hearts
Never even torn apart

On the hospital floor
You don't spare a prayer

Crying under a chandelier
Breathing in the cold air

All the walls in your mansion
You only hang logic and reason

All these things but I only have bits
I fear I may die like this

Tongues of Flowers

DLL

"Artisan of Dreams"

Artisan of dreams
You are the tempter of things
All of my desires
You dangle from a string

You shouldn't have read
Papers I should've shred
You couldn't have guessed
Writings of all you've ever said

And from the corner of my eye
I couldn't help but see
The prettiest fellow
Staring at me

Artisan of dreams
You are the tempter of things
You hold all of me
I'm hung from your strings

DLL

"The Pit"

Every time I try to get up, I can't stay up
Cause I wonder why
I wasn't enough when all I did was try

But now I don't know peace
Tell me why
I didn't know the price would be so high

Tongues of Flowers

This guilt was never ever
Supposed to be mine
It's eating me alive

DLL

CHAPTER FORTY-TWO

My Interview with Julian Wallace.

Seven by Taylor Swift

There was only one person I thought might talk to me.

Julian Wallace.

Julian and I went to elementary school together, though we didn't pay each other any mind until I went to 6th grade and Julian into 8th. We moved in with one of my mom's boyfriends, Craig, who was Julian's next-door neighbor.

Julian ran up next to me as I was walking to school. "My momma said I gotta walk you to school," he said. I looked down at him, he was much shorter than me at the time. He ran his hand over the top of his afro and looked ahead. I remember thinking he was good looking.

"I don't need you to walk with me!" I declared.

Tongues of Flowers

"Well, that's too damn bad!" he said, marching ahead. I stopped in my tracks and folded my arms. "Oh, c'mon. We're headed to the same place anyway, mine as well walk together."

I rolled my eyes. "Whatever."

Despite my annoyance, Julian and I became good friends, and we established a routine. We would put together our coins and walk to the dollar store after school to get a 2-liter soda to share. After that, we explored the canal, the houses across the street had docks. One of those houses was owned by an older lady who would let us use her kayak. So, we would get on the kayak with our 2-liter Cheerwine and look for critters.

One day I came to school acting quiet, I was upset because Craig was drinking again and I was paying the price.

"When I grow up, I'm gon' buy a big ol' house, one of the fancy ones with a dock. You can come live in it too if you want," Julian said.

"I'm gon' buy the house next to yours, and it'll be twice as big and have an indoor pool!" I teased. He dropped his jaw and splashed me with water. "But if you're nice I might let ya live in the basement," I said.

"Woah!"

"Well, just a corner. Don't get too excited, Julian."

The summer before 9th grade Craig kicked all of us out of the house. We went to stay with one of my mother's coworkers on the other side of town. Julian got a scholarship to transfer to a fancy prep school, and that was the end of that.

It just so happened; it was the same prep school Ted went to. So, I thought Julian might be able to help me.

Tongues of Flowers

We met at a cafe. He had finally surpassed me in height, and he looked so neat with his flashy gold watch and tan turtleneck. He sat across from Eleo and me. He was working in finance.

"Hey, you're that cop that's always poking around," Julian said, pointing to Eleo.

"Guilty as charged," he said.

"It's a long story, Julian."

"Okay, well, anyway, it's been so long, Alba. I've always wondered what happened to you. What are you doing these days? Do you still write?" he asked. He turned to Eleo. "She used to always carry around this little black notebook with flower stickers, I tried to read it so many times but she guarded it with her life." Julian laughed.

"I plan to get back to writing again, but I have to sort through this thing first, it's actually why I reached out to you… you went to high school with Ted Yoshida right?"

"He was a couple of grades ahead of me, but yeah, he went to the academy with me. You two were a thing for a while, right?" he asked.

"Yeah, I don't know exactly what you heard, but it didn't go well. If you talk to him, please don't mention that you saw me," I said. He agreed. "What do you know about him?" I asked.

"I mean, we weren't close or anything, mostly just had mutual friends. He was always a calm, nice guy, and obviously insanely smart, not super social, though like I said, we did have some mutual friends and so we hung out a few times, and yeah, like I said, nice guy."

"Did you ever meet his twin brother? Lee?" Eleo asked.

Tongues of Flowers

"No, I never met him. I heard he was in and out of psychiatric hospitals growing up so his family kept him pretty isolated. When he turned 18 he was kicked out or maybe he just left, but he ended up dying of an overdose soon after. It was sad, but Ted's family had a private funeral and yeah, Ted didn't like to talk about him, and no one ever really got to know Lee, so I don't know much about him."

"Do you know any of the specifics surrounding the overdose? What had he overdosed on? The location? Anything?" I asked.

"No, I'm sorry, I don't. If I think of anything I'll let you know, though," Julian said.

As we said our goodbyes Julian hugged me. "I'm having a party tonight, by the way. I live near the canal we went to as a kid, on the nice side though, like I said I would. But yeah, you should come. I'll text you the address."

I didn't give him a sure answer.

"I think I should go, he and Ted had a lot of mutual friends, I might be able to find someone who can help, especially with the alcohol that'll be in their systems," I said.

"You think they're still around?" Eleo said, holding the door open for me.

"Yeah, these were the types of guys that peaked in high school. They're still in Hampstead."

Eleo grinned and shook his head. "You are honest as ever, Alba."

I feel like you're opening doors, Lord. Don't stop.

CHAPTER FORTY-THREE

Spirits Don't Lie

Mr. Brightside by The Killers

"I never knew you were a hat guy," I said to Eleo, who was in the driver's seat, glaring at me from under his gray baseball cap.

"It's a disguise. I'm not kidding when I tell you I've been harassing these people for the better part of three years."

It was true. He even rented a studio in Hampstead so he could come on his days off.

We parked up the street from Julian's house, which was already littered with cars and front yard pow-wows. "Well, that's a very creative disguise," I said, flicking the tip of his hat.

"Yeah, well, I left my high heels in Raleigh."

We walked up the driveway, passing a beer pong tournament and a herd of girls in wet shirts. As we entered the house we were met with a combination of scents; vape juice, sweat, and spilled beer, namely.

Tongues of Flowers

"Hey, you see that blonde girl by the fireplace?" Eleo said into my ear.

"Yeah, that's Clarisse Newborne, she married a military guy and moved around the same time I did, I think," I said, watching Clarissa twirl her long blonde hair.

"She dated Ted in high school, I recognize her from some of his old pictures, I could never get in contact with her though. You should try to talk to her," he said.

I made my way over and greeted Clarisse. I could see in her eyes that she had no idea who I was. "We were in pageants together," I lied. She squealed and jumped up and down in her purple cocktail dress, pretending she suddenly remembered me. I gestured her towards a quiet doorway.

"This is going to sound strange, but we both dated Ted Yoshida, and I was wondering what you know about his brother," I said.

"Ted? Oh, honey, that was back in high school, you can have him! He was a nice boy but I heard he went crazy after his wife died, so you probably won't want to bother," she said, waving at someone behind me.

"I don't want him, I am suspicious of him, though. Do you know anything about his brother, Lee?" I asked.

"Just that he was a bad seed, one day Ted got a call while we were at lunch that Lee was being checked into a psychiatric hospital because his parents found him with a bunch of pills and a suicide note. He hardly batted an eye, said it was always something with Lee," she explained.

"That didn't seem a bit cynical to you?" I asked.

Tongues of Flowers

She smiled and placed her hand on my cheek. "Oh, honey, it's been so great talking to you! I gotta head over there, I promised I'd catch up with Kenzie and she's all by herself over there. Why don't you talk to Bono, he's in the basement," she said.

"Bono's here? I thought he moved out west?" I asked.

"He's back in town visiting family," she said, walking away.

I made eye contact with Eleo and gestured toward the basement. He quickly caught up to me as we headed down the crowded stairs into a basement with colorful lights. "Did she tell you anything important?" he asked.

"Sort of, she said Ted's old best friend is here."

"Bono? I've been calling him, he lives out in Colorado," Eleo said, just as we both looked up to see Bono on the couch on his phone. "You want me to get this one?" he asked. I shook my head.

"I've been out of the game long enough."

Bono's green eyes looked me up and down before I had even approached him. "You're comin' to talk to me?" he asked, gesturing for me to join him on the couch. "You're too cute, what's your name? You look so familiar," he said, putting his arm behind me. His breath smelled like gin. It reminded me of Ted.

"Thanks, yeah, I used to live here, we had some mutual friends, I think," I said, slightly leaning my face away from his face.

"Yeah?"

"Yeah, like Ted Yoshida." Bono's smile faded when he heard Ted's name. "Did you ever meet his brother?" I asked.

Tongues of Flowers

"Why?" he asked, removing his arm from around me. Before I could answer his eyes narrowed, he pointed a finger in my face and yelled, "you're that crazy b'tch!"

Eleo came out of nowhere, removing Bono's hand from my face, I instinctually stood up next to him.

"Who the hell are you?!"

"Don't worry about it man, just don't come at her like that again," Eleo said. Bono stood up, face to face with Eleo, who stood his ground calmly. Bono was very drunk, but not too much to realize that he didn't stand a chance against Eleo. He let out a stream of swears as he walked off.

"We should go," I said.

"I won't argue with you on that one."

As we were heading to the car we were stopped by a man with kind eyes. "Wait! I know who you are!" he called out.

"We're leaving, we don't want any trouble," I assured him.

"My name is Hakeem, I was a friend of Ted's. You're the cop, right? You tried to talk to me a few months ago, I said no because I was scared, but I recognize you now that you two are together, Ted made those videos about you," Hakeem said.

"What he said in those videos wasn't true, you know," Eleo said.

"I believe you, and I think we should talk, but not here."

We followed Hakeem to his car. "I'm only going to say these things once, and then I want no part of this ever again," he said. We agreed. Eleo pressed the record button on his phone.

CHAPTER FORTY-FOUR

The Transcript of Hakeem Brown

Stick Season by Noah Kahan

Hakeem: Well I guess I should start from the beginning.

Eleo: Okay, whenever you're ready.

Hakeem: I was one of the developers that helped Ted with Food4U. We only ever communicated remotely, but when he opened the headquarters in Charlotte I moved there. Ted was an introvert, he mostly worked from his home in Hampstead. But he came to the headquarters for a meeting I happened to be in, I was quick on my feet, which amused him, I suppose. We went for drinks after.

Eleo: Just the two of you?

Hakeem: Yeah, just the two of us. He told me he was dating this girl, Diamond, that she was beautiful and intelligent, and that he was thinking about proposing. He started coming into the office more, and we spent a lot of time together, developing, creating, dreaming… months went by and he kept saying he was thinking about proposing and then looking at me to gauge my reaction, I always kept very quiet, until one day…

Alba: Are you all right?

Hakeem: Yes, my apologies. I have never told anyone this besides my priest.

Alba: You don't have to…

Hakeem: Yes, I do. So this one day Ted said he's thinking about proposing to Diamond and he asked what I thought, I finally just told him I didn't think he should, he asked why and I just leaned over and kissed him. And he kissed me back. I had never done anything like that before. I left rather abruptly, first to confession and then home.

Hakeem: He came to my apartment that evening, he told me to stop dodging his calls and that… he loved me, that he would be okay with Diamond but not truly happy. I told him, "no human person can make you happy if you aren't," and I closed the door. I sat against the door in tears the rest of the night, listening to him plead on the other side of the door.

Alba: Ted's bisexual?

Hakeem: Ted is gay if you ask me.

Alba: Sorry, I believe you that just… I'm very surprised by all this. Continue, sorry.

Hakeem: I understand. But anyway, I avoided him as much as possible. We still worked at the same company but mostly avoided each other, just occasional glances of longing. My desires were at war with one another, I almost told him not to marry her. I went to their wedding, I sat in the back, and I really thought I was going to stand when they said, "speak now." But I didn't, and I left before he even saw me.

Hakeem: From then on, I prayed for nothing but the best for him and Diamond. The next time I saw him I was working late and he came into my office in tears, locking the door behind him. He begged for my help, he said he had been keeping a secret and that it was tormenting him.

Eleo: What was the secret, Hakeem?

Hakeem: His brother, Lee, had not died of an overdose at 18. He was still alive. His family made up the story and shunned Lee out of shame because of his drug use. But of course, Ted worried about him still, so he tracked him down to Doure, a halfway house in South Carolina. He wanted me to go with him. I don't know why he asked me, but I agreed to go.

Alba: Oh my gosh.

Hakeem: Yeah, yeah… so we went to the halfway house and met Lee, they were identical but so different, Lee was a mess, it was heart-wrenching. But he seemed receptive to help, despite his physical condition, I actually found him to be quite charming, even more so than Ted.

Hakeem: On the way home Ted thanked me for going and he seemed very committed to helping Lee. Over the next few weeks he even brought Lee to his house, he and Diamond started helping him to get back on his feet, he apparently sobered up and was doing well. Of course, Ted swore me to secrecy, he didn't want his parents to find out about Lee.

Tongues of Flowers

Hakeem: Then out of nowhere, Ted stopped going into the office. He dodged my calls. I texted him asking about Lee, he texted back saying Lee overdosed and died. I was shocked, of course, he had been giving such positive reports until then. I went to see him to see if he was okay but he didn't answer. Two days later, Diamond killed herself. Ted hasn't spoken to me since any of this.

Alba: Lee and Diamond's deaths were two days apart? And nobody besides you and Ted even know about Lee's actual overdose?

Hakeem: I don't know. I've told you all I know.

Alba: I'm sorry, I don't mean to bombard you. I'm sorry you went through all of that, it must have been… just awful to go through and carry by yourself.

Eleo: Yeah, that couldn't have been easy.

Hakeem: It's all right, I know you have been through quite a lot yourself with no support. I don't know what exactly you're looking for being back in Hampstead, but I hope what I told you helps you find it.

Alba: Thank you, Hakeem.

Eleo: What about you, Hakeem? Why are you back in Hampstead, you live in Charlotte, right?

Hakeem: I'm actually going to be joining a monastery, I'm finding closure with my past before I leave.

Eleo: That's incredible, what made you decide to do that?

Hakeem: I have experienced a lot of pleasure in life now, and I've come to the conclusion that there is nothing that can be found in this world that compares to Christ. I just want to spend my life in quiet reflection of His brilliance, and to write about it.

Tongues of Flowers

Alba: I wish I were as strong as you.

Hakeem: No, you don't. I'm actually quite weak to the entanglements of this world. That's why I'm leaving them behind for Someone that is safe to carry my weakness.

Alba: Did you love Ted?

Hakeem: Yes, I did. It saddens me to know what he's been through, and to hear that he's changed and gone off the deep end, it scares me to think what grievous sins he's committed by now. I've seen bits and pieces of his online persona, I don't recognize that man. But anyway, I finally love him enough to set him free, yes, sometimes our consequences are the only blades sharp enough to cut through our nooses.

CHAPTER FORTY-FIVE

Doure's House for the Lonesome

Viva Las Vengeance by Panic! At The Disco

"So Ted's gay?" Eleo said, breaking the silence as he pulled into my brother's driveway.

"I guess, I mean, I don't know."

"Did you ever…"

"Yeah, we did. Especially at the beginning, but towards the end we stopped, I assumed it was because he was sleeping with Yana," I paused and felt the heat rise to my cheeks. I looked at Eleo, he was listening attentively but looked away with a flushed face when I looked at him.

"That would explain why Diamond had an affair, if Ted wasn't, uh, fulfilling that," he said.

"Maybe. I don't know, he really seemed into it. But I don't know. I think we should go to that halfway house in South Carolina that Hakeem mentioned where Lee was, see if we can find out more about Lee's death," I said.

"Do you think the affair might have been…" he trailed off.

"With Lee?" I finished his sentence for him.

"Yeah."

"I mean, if Hakeem was being truthful, that would be an explanation for why their deaths were so close together," I said. "We need to go to Doure."

The next morning I sat on the porch, waiting for Eleo to pick me up.

"So you're going on an overnight trip with a guy, but he's just a friend?" Loo asked.

"It's a work thing," I said.

"You're unemployed," he crooned. I shrugged. It made me happy hearing him talk like an older brother, it reminded me of when we were young.

Eleo pulled in and walked to the steps to grab my bag for me. The boys exchanged an awkward handshake proceeded by a death glare from Loo. "I thought it was just you two?" Loo asked.

"Oh yeah, she called shotgun, but maybe you can barter with her," Eleo said.

"Her?" I asked. My eyes narrowed and I saw a familiar face in the passenger seat. "Donnie!" I shouted, running to her. She opened the door and held out her arms.

Donnie had just finished touring with Loae Daegle as her show photographer, so she was visiting through the holidays before heading back to LA. She said she was still writing music; it just wasn't her bill's passion of choice. "I have this growing suspicion that things will never turn out like we expect them to," she said.

We got to Doure. We wisely had Eleo wear his cop uniform, with that it took very little convincing for the receptionist, who looked too young to buy a bottle of wine, to give us Lee's belongings.

"Thank you for these, if you don't mind me asking, do you remember him?" I queried.

"Tall, Japanese-American guy, right?" she said, barely looking up from her phone.

"Yes," I said.

"I remember him."

"Did he ever have any visitors?" Eleo asked.

"Not really, some people down by the bars might know him. But the only visitor I remember was his twin brother who came by with a friend, and then he came by again and took Lee with him, but then Lee was back a few days later, he said he got in a fight with his brother, don't know about what," she said.

"And then what?" I asked.

"And then he was just in and out for a week, haven't seen him in years now, though. We're not allowed to get rid of their stuff though, they had a lawsuit and ever since won't let us throw anything out."

"You didn't hear anything about an overdose?" Eleo asked.

"No, I haven't heard anything, did he? That's a shame."

I briefly looked through the bag of Lee's belongings as we headed back to Eleo's car. Just clothes and a lighter.

Tongues of Flowers

"Maybe tomorrow we can go talk to some of the locals at the bar scene," I said. Eleo agreed.

But as we were driving Donnie started searching the bag of Lee's belongings and she gasped.

"What?" Eleo and I both asked. I looked in the rearview mirror, she had her hand over her mouth and held a crumpled-up piece of paper.

"It's a letter."

CHAPTER FORTY-SIX

Votre Amour

The Blower's Daughter by Damien Rice

Lee,

Oh, Lee. Please don't hate me for saying this, but I'm in torment, and it's because of you. Yet the only remaining happiness is you, I feel nothing outside of you, there isn't any pleasure left to be found. I think of nothing but you every single day and night. There is something in you that looks eerily like me, and that's a scary thought, I've never seen something so ugly. I want you.

He's in the bed as we speak. I'm looking at his head, why could I never climb inside of it? Why could I never break through? Why did he never really see me? You're identical, why is it that you look so different?

I will come to the shack on the 21st as you requested, and then I never want to see that dreadful place ever again. We can go anywhere, think of somewhere he never would. I don't care where. I have to get

Tongues of Flowers

out of here. I cannot do this any longer, living like the dead. I need you.

Votre Amour

CHAPTER FORTY-SEVEN

You Know That I Know That You Know

In Your Hands by Citipointe Worship, Joel Ramsey

"So, just to clarify, we're all on the same page that there's no way anyone other than Diamond wrote that letter, right?" Donnie said, plopping on one of the hotel twin beds.

"Right," Eleo said, quietly unfolding the pull-out couch.

"So let me just word vomit a theory here," I said, sitting up in the other twin bed. "Ted stopped sleeping with Diamond after a while because he was battling his sexuality. So when Ted brings Lee around to try and help him, Lee and Diamond start up an affair. Ted finds out somehow, and he goes off the rails, probably a combination of mental illness which seems to have been genetic and his anxiety over his sexuality being exposed. So, Ted kills Lee. Diamond is so devastated by Lee's death, that she commits suicide."

"That has to be it," Eleo said.

"We need more proof though," Donnie added.

Tongues of Flowers

"Well, let's get some sleep, we have a couple of days before Eleo has to return to work, we can go talk to the locals in the morning," I said.

I went to brush my teeth and Donnie popped into the bathroom. "What's going on with you and Eleo?" she whispered.

"Nothing, I mean, there was something before I left, but it's been years, I think he's over it and moved on, which is fine. I don't think either of us expected to see each other again," I said.

"So, you don't have feelings for him anymore?" Donnie asked.

"Well, I mean, I probably always will, I don't know. I can't help it. I'm happy by myself though," I stammered.

Donnie smirked. "All right then."

"But hey, do you know of anything ever happening with him and Leah-Jane after I left?" I asked.

Donnie laughed. "No, Leah-Jane tried, but he rejected her. Eleo has not been with anyone, at least nothing serious enough for me to have heard about it, since you left."

"Oh."

She smiled again and patted my back before walking out. It seemed trivial to be thinking about something like love at a time like that, but he looked so perfect reading on the sofa bed. And I had this indescribable feeling of belonging when he was around.

But the gravity of the mission at hand quickly returned.

I prayed fervently that night, for nearly an hour until I fell asleep.

Lord,

Tongues of Flowers

Please show me the way. I'm fully dependent on You; I know that You know the truth, and You are honestly the only one I fully trust with that. Please show me, I trust You. Don't let me be misled, show me where to go next, please, Lord. I love you, either way. If You don't show me, I know You have Your reasons and we will have quite the talk and unveiling in heaven but I am begging you, please show me the truth, above all, show me Your glory.

Amen

CHAPTER FORTY-EIGHT

The Language of Dreams

Firm Foundation by Maverick City

That morning I jumped out of bed, exasperated. Before I could even process the dream, I knew it was of great importance, somehow. I sketched out what I saw. A wooden shack littered with autumn leaves, and yellow flowers covering the floors.

"Eleo! Do you know these flowers? They're supposed to be yellow, if that helps," I asked, leaning next to the sofa bed, and pointing to my sketch. He rubbed his eyes and leaned upward.

"Yeah, that's yellow jessamine, South Carolina's state flower, actually," Eleo said.

"I need to call Skipper," I said.

I sent the information over digitally and Skipper was able to locate a shack in SC that looked just like my sketch, it was hidden deep within a state park not far from our hotel, since Doure had already brought us to Greenville, SC.

Tongues of Flowers

"How did you know there was a shed like that in South Carolina?" Donnie asked.

"Like I said, it was just from my dream," I said.

"Yeah, but like, how did your subconscious know?" she asked.

"It didn't, there was no way I could've known about this shed. I was praying last night for God to show me where to go next, and then I felt this sense of peace and slipped into a deep sleep and He showed me this shack and I could just feel it was Him showing me," I explained.

Donnie stared at me wide-eyed. Eleo looked at me from the side, sporting a grin that gave me butterflies.

CHAPTER FORTY-NINE

Me and You and All of These Ashes

Meet Me at Our Spot by WILLOW

Donnie and I walked arm in arm as the three of us trudged through the state park, following Eleo's map.

"Go talk to him," Donnie whispered.

"No! I don't want to!" I mouthed.

"Eleo, I don't think you know what you're doing with that map," Donnie yelled. Eleo looked back, shooting her a sly look. "But don't worry, I'll send Alba to help you," she said, pushing me into Eleo against my will.

"Sorry," I said, removing my hands from his back. He looked down at me, holding back a laugh and shaking his head.

"Despite Donnie's lack of faith in me, I actually think we're close, that might be it over that hill, I'm not sure if you see it, that run-down little thing," he said, pointing ahead.

Tongues of Flowers

"Wow, you did it, I should have had more faith in you," I teased.

"Bet you never wavered in your faith in Mateo's sense of geography," he teased back.

"How did you know about Mateo?" I asked.

"You should know by now my Abuela is a gossip."

"There wasn't really anything going on with us," I said.

His eyebrows rose. "It's okay if there was, I figured you'd moved on."

"Well, I figured you would have long been married to Leah-Jane by now," I rebutted.

"It was never going to be Leah-Jane," he said, a smirk on his face as if that should have been obvious.

"No?" I blushed.

"No." His eyes gleamed.

Our conversation was cut short as I fell through the leaves and down a dark hole. "Alba!" Eleo called out after me, I could see Donnie run over and poke her head over the top of the steep hole.

"What do we do?" Donnie asked Eleo.

"You go get help," Eleo said, he then jumped down the hole.

"What? Eleo!" Donnie called out as Eleo slid down after me.

"Eleo! Why would you do that!" I yelled, grabbing onto his shoulders.

"I don't know! I was just worried!" The hole was small, so his face was just inches from mine.

"Well, great, now we're both stuck," I said.

Tongues of Flowers

"Yeah, but that's kind of how it is with us, right?"

Before I could answer, a terrible smell hit my nose, and I suddenly became aware of my surroundings. "Eleo, what are we on top of?"

We both felt the hard texture under us.

"Oh my gosh," I whispered.

"Bones," he said.

CHAPTER FIFTY

Star Littered Views from the Terrace

Call It What You Want by Taylor Swift

The local authorities were called, and it seemed we were finally being taken seriously.

The bones were being taken in for forensic testing, so there was nothing left for us to do but go back to the hotel and rest.

Eleo and I found ourselves unwinding with take-outs on the balcony after Donnie passed out.

"What other gossip did your abuela impart to you while we were apart?" I asked.

"Hmm, well I heard you got your GED, congratulations, by the way," he said.

I laughed and raised my glass. "Thanks."

"And I heard you can drive, very poorly," he laughed.

Tongues of Flowers

"Well very poorly isn't not at all, so, I'm content," I replied.

"And I heard that you matured a lot, and that you're known as being close to God."

"She said that?" I asked, my jaw slipping.

"Yeah, so did Maria. And seeing you now, well, I can tell," he said.

"Well, that means a lot coming from you. I've always thought you had the closest relationship to Him of anyone I know," I confessed.

"Yeah?"

"Yeah, I did." I paused and took a deep breath. "I guess that's why I loved you," I added.

He looked ahead toward the star-littered sky with an amused smile. "And that's as good an explanation as any as to why I have never stopped loving you," he said.

CHAPTER FIFTY-ONE

The Call of Calls

If I told You This Was Killing Me by The Juliana Theory

Weeks went by without any update from forensics. Eleo went back to work in Raleigh. I enrolled in community college classes and started waiting table's part time while living with Loo and my mother in Hampstead. I also started attending a small church near my brother's house.

"One of the ladies at my church works for the police department, she says they're hiring," I told Eleo as we perused through an old thrift store. He had been visiting me in Hampstead regularly. I had also visited Raleigh for dinner with him, Nia, and Skipper.

"I'll have to look into that," he agreed. We had been talking about him moving to Hampstead.

"Look how pretty!" I exclaimed, reaching for an emerald teapot on the top shelf. He wrapped his arm around my waist and kissed my cheek before lowering it for me.

Tongues of Flowers

My phone started ringing.

I took the call.

It was the forensics lab.

"Yes ma'am, we thought you should know before the outlets do, that one of the remains was identified as belonging to Ted Yoshida," the man said.

"You mean Lee Yoshida? Ted is his brother, the film director," I explained.

"No, ma'am. As it turns out Lee Yoshida is alive and well, Ted Yoshida died several years ago."

CHAPTER FIFTY-TWO

Yoshida

John Wayne Gacy by Sufjan Stevens

Lee Yoshida's parents first noticed their son was different when he began developing weapons of torture to use on his pets in the first grade.

He had an infamous temper. Throwing cartons of milk at the grocery store clerk. Using his mother's lipstick to create an illusion of fake blood on the wall. Tripping his grandmother with her cane because she suggested he eat his vegetables.

He saw every sort of therapist and was on every medication money could buy.

But ever curious, was the case of Lee Yoshida.

While Lee was overtaken by a compulsion to harm, there were moments in his life when he desired to do what was good.

In 5th grade, Lee and Ted were playing with a neighbor. Lee seldom was allowed around other children, but he had been behaving well recently, so his parents allowed it.

Tongues of Flowers

The neighbor's name was Tracy Stevens. She called Ted a slur. Ted cried.

Lee saw this as his chance to stick up for his brother, which he figured would lead to a bond between them. Lee murdered Tracy Stevens with his bare hands. This was his first murder. His family made it all go away but kept Lee more isolated than ever.

He both commemorated and mourned the incident by drawing a crayon portrait of his victim. He also kept a lock of Tracy's hair, he could give no reason as to why. Years later, he put it in the manhole near the shack in the woods.

His entire childhood he struggled to understand how even when he tried to do right, he did wrong.

Meanwhile, Ted stayed busy at school and with extracurriculars to avoid his brother. Not that he needed to, most of the time Lee was away at some sort of psychiatric facility. Ted also felt an immense pressure to be perfect, to compensate for his brother's wickedness.

Lee's brain began to shut down as he struggled to cope with his past decisions and state of being. In high school, he gained access to recreational drugs.

His parents, overwhelmed by shame and fear, shunned Lee, paying him to stay away from Hampstead. They fabricated a story about him dying of a drug overdose.

Lee was cruising through a life of mindless self-indulgence until Ted, overwhelmed with guilt from letting his brother leave, came and got him out of Doure Halfway House. He brought him into his home.

Lee and Diamond immediately had tension. She wrote about it non-stop in her journals, which Lee read, leading to the affair.

Tongues of Flowers

If you were to ask Lee, he would tell you that to this day, Diamond Lee is the only person he ever loved.

Diamond had grown to resent Ted. He was emotionally closed off and lacked interest in her. She was intrigued by Lee.

Perhaps Diamond mistook Lee's destructive and impetuous behaviors as passionate and mesmeric. Or perhaps she saw what Lee did, but she didn't take it for what it was. Regardless of her reasons, the evidence is clear... Diamond loved Lee.

And Lee would do anything to ensure that didn't change.

So, he killed Ted.

Lee presented Ted's body to Diamond as she stood before him at the shack. Diamond gave every possible reaction in the 24 hours that proceeded. Relief. Joy. Shame. Guilt. Fear.

Eventually, reality set in, she truly saw Lee, and she could not bear it. So, she took her life.

Lee went into survival mode.

He took on the name of his deceased brother, Ted Yoshida, and created a new persona that was a combination of the two. He cut off anyone who would have been able to tell the difference. He spent his days blowing through Ted's money and drinking with the guys he had always wanted to be like, Chad Moore especially, and he began sleeping around with the most attractive women the east coast had to offer.

Then he met me, to him, I represented some sort of hybrid, made up of what was and what would be. I could never be Diamond. But I was there. I could be his. He just needed a constant, someone to believe his new persona, something to ground him, someone to need him.

Tongues of Flowers

But as it turned out, he couldn't make me unhuman, I was not an object, as much as he wanted me to be one.

And then Yana entered the picture. She had an ethereal sort of feel. He romanticized her in every possible way, he hoped he could grow to love her.

Once Ted fabricated the story about Eleo and I harassing him, he found he had accidentally garnered sympathy from the crowds and fell in love with their praises. He dove into the spotlight. He even forgot about Yana, redirecting his compulsions toward garnering as much praise as possible from the masses.

This preoccupied him for a time.

But then the crowds began to grow tired of him. It was around that same time he saw Yana with her husband, Jonabee, at a premier, and something within him switched.

Her charmed her, pulling out every trick he had. And to Lee's credit, she did indeed turn out to be a great deal darker than Diamond, though he still didn't love Yana, in fact, his emotions were filtering away by the day. He pushed harder.

Lee and Yana plotted together. She convinced Jonabee to take out a large life insurance policy, while Lee took care of the dirtier work. He threw his body into that same hole by the shack and went back to start his new life with Yana.

What Lee didn't realize, likely because he could not view me as a human being, was that he had not tied me, a loose end, up. And I pulled that thread until all he had weaved came undone.

Epilogue

I Found You by Zach Webb

12 Years Later.

Jug, our black kitten, greeted us on our white sheets.

"How was your day, detective?" I asked, peering up from my glasses.

"Doctor," he said, greeting me with a kiss. "It was all right, how about yours?" Eleo asked.

"Well, Jen called today. She wants me to be a consultant for the film," I said.

"Consultant? You should be the one writing the script," he said.

"Just because I was there?" I asked.

"Because you're brilliant," he laughed, kissing my cheek. "Because you're a professor, you're imaginative, and pleasant, and strategic, and lovely, and should I go on?" he asked, wrapping his arms around me, and burying his face into my side.

"I love you, Eleo."

"I love you, Alba."

Soundtrack

"The Widow" by The Mars Volta

"Frankly, Mr. Shankly" by The Smiths

"As It Was" by Harry Styles

"Dreams" by The Cranberries

"First Day of My Life" by Bright Eyes

"Lucky One (Taylor's Version)" by Taylor Swift

"Mystery of Love" by Sufjan Stevens

"Innuendo and out the Other" by Cave In

"The Lakes (Original Version)" by Taylor Swift

"Pretty Woman" by Roy Orbison

"Who I Am Hates Who I've Been" by Reliant K

"Freaks" by Surfs Curse

"The World is Ugly" by My Chemical Romance

"To Be Alone with You" by Sufjan Stevens

Tongues of Flowers

"And I Told Them I Invented Times New Roman" by Dance Gavin Dance

"Fast Car" by Tracy Chapman

"Everywhere" by Fleetwood Mac

"Heart Like Yours" by Willamette Stone

"Your Best American Girl" by Mitski

"Without You" by RIDERS, Circuit Rider Music

"Late Night Talking" by Harry Styles

"Duvet" by Boa

"Moon Song" by Phoebe Bridgers

"But You Won't Love a Ghost" by Emarosa

"It's Safe to Say you Dig the Backseat" by Dance Gavin Dance

"Me and my Husband" by Mitski

"Carry Me Ohio" by Sun Kil Moon

"Ivy" (non-explicit version) by Taylor Swift

"Your Love is Like" by Rick Pino

"Play Date" by Melanie Martinez

"On the Way Down" by Ryan Cabrera

"I'll Never Let You Go" by Zach Webb

"Out Loud" by Scarypoolparty

"It's a Wonderful Life" by John Lucas

"Gold Rush" by Taylor Swift

Tongues of Flowers

"Egypt" by Cory Asbury

"Lobo-hombre en Paris" by La Union

"Carolina in My Mind" by John Denver

"'Tis the Damn Season" by Taylor Swift

"Dancing With Our Hands Tied" by Taylor Swift

"Illicit Affairs" by Taylor Swift

"Seven" by Taylor Swift

"Mr. Brightside" by The Killers

"Stick Season" by Noah Kahan

"Viva Las Vengeance" by Panic! At The Disco

"The Blower's Daughter" by Damien Rice

"In Your Hands" by Citipointe Worship, Joel Ramsey

"Firm Foundation" by Maverick City

"Meet Me At Our Spot" by THE ANXIETY, WILLOW, Tyler Cole

"Call It What You Want" by Taylor Swift

"If I Told You This Was Killing Me" by The Juliana Theory

"John Wayne Gacy, Jr." by Sufjan Stevens

"I Found You" by Zach Webb

Dear Reader

Well, what did you think?

I will let you in on a secret (you have been piddling around my brain the last couple of hours, so it is safe to say we are friends). Here is the secret: I cried while writing the chapter entitled *Stay with Me*.

(Spoiler alert, for those who skipper ahead)

I cried specifically when Eleo was holding Alba as she cried in the bed after finally leaving Ted.

First, I cried because I remembered how it felt to finally be out of a relationship that I had spent years in against my better judgement. I cried because I remembered how I so desperately wanted to be held. I wanted to cry into the arms of someone who would be honest and gentle, someone I could speak freely to without worrying that they would lash out at me in return.

Then, I cried even harder, because I realized I did have that, and I still do. During that difficult time, I was hanging onto God by a thread, but He never lost His grip on me. There is nowhere too dark that he could not see me, and there was never anywhere too deep that He would not have caught me. And even when I ran or hid, He knew how the story would end.

Tongues of Flowers

Yes, God is my comfort, I feel His wings around me when it's 2am and I'm crying over the past. And He is honest with me, even when it hurts, because the truth sets us free. And He has been ever so gentle with me, when I got myself in messes against my better judgement. He's brought me to a much better place, and our intimacy is growing deeper every day. Telling me He isn't real at this point would be like telling me my mom or dog aren't real, it would be an absurd notion at this point.

Now, just a warning, I still a massive recipient of grace, I am going to do more stupid things. And you will too. You do not have to go through it alone. And being praised as "*a cool girl*" or avoiding "*I told you so*" is not worth staying in a dangerous situation.

You were made for more than that.

After all, there is a specific mission at hand to which you have been called.

Until next time,

Lynn S.E.